THE SAGITTAN CHRONICLES: THE PREQUEL

All In

by Ariele Sieling

AUTHOR'S NOTE

Dear Reader,

Welcome to the Sagittan Chronicles. Those of you who have read the other books in the series—thank you! For those of you who are first dipping in your toes, I thought a few details might be helpful.

This is a prequel, meaning it happens about thirty years before the events of the first book of the series, *The Wounded World*. That said, the people of Sagitta are an old race and live much longer than humans. Quin, the main character, is 223 years old, while John is 198. Jo is a little bit younger—188. Sagittans can live to be 700 – 800 years old. In this book, Quin is currently serving in the military as a Door Specialist, while John is a mathematician at the Globe. Both are still at the beginning of their careers. You will meet them both in the other books.

The story is set primarily in Pomegranate City on the planet Sagitta, and revolves around a piece of technology called a Door. A Door is a device that allows you to leap large distances of space in a single step with little to no time passing. Doors were developed many millennia ago, but in recent centuries have been taken control of by the Globe, an organization with close ties to the Sagittan government. Doors create security concerns, so owning one without permission is now technically illegal, though many families have secretly held onto them as heirlooms.

I plan on building and growing this universe for a long time, so if you find the Sagittan Chronicles interesting, there are plenty more to come (including the first few books in the series that are already published!). I hope you enjoy the story. If not, that's cool too—not every story is for everyone. If you do like it, please consider writing a review on Amazon or Goodreads.

Sincerely,
Ariele Sieling, author

CHAPTER 1

Quin stood on a dais overlooking a large room. Beside him sat a small table with a marble bowl on top, covered in a layer of dust. Two knives, also made of marble, lay beside the bowl. The room itself boasted pillars along each wall and a high ceiling, detailed with a chipped and peeling painting of a woman with long silver hair and wings the color of midnight. Cracked and faded stained glass windows cast shadows of crimson and gold on the floor.

But what riveted his attention was row after row of chairs, the once-elegant seats now covered in grime with the wooden legs and backs cracking and bent—each occupied by a figure of bones. Skeleton upon skeleton filled every single chair from the front of the room to the back. Rags draped from the bones; arms hung from the shoulders. Some skulls had fallen and rolled across the floor; some chairs contained nothing more than a pile of ribs and phalanges with the occasional clavicle or patella mixed in. Jewels lay scattered across the room, necklaces hung in rib cages, and rings had slipped from their owners' fingers and rolled across the floor.

Quin stepped forward. The sound of his feet echoed in the room so loudly it startled him. The high ceilings and flat walls were ideal for echoes, and he felt the muscles in his neck tense as he moved past the empty eyes and towards the exit. It was eerie, as if the silence and empty eye sockets seemed to watch his every move.

Except for his breathing and echoing footfalls, he heard no other sounds. He thought maybe this place had once been a temple of some sort, a place of worship. But no one had maintained it for a long time—and who would, with an audience made of bones? Paint peeled from the walls; broken bricks and pieces of plaster littered the floor; dust covered every surface.

Who were they? Why did they die? Perhaps he had landed in an odd form of cemetery, where mourners placed the bodies in the chairs where they slowly wasted away. But why was there a Door in that room? Why would anyone choose to come here? No, more likely there had been a catastrophe—something that had caused all these people to die at once.

The hallway he stepped into was in much the same state of disrepair. He moved slowly, one hand resting close to the gun he carried on his belt, the other holding a walking stick designed to look inconspicuous while also strong enough to function as a weapon. Behind him, a hover camera followed, capturing everything.

The hallway ended at a large wooden door carved with depictions of five-leafed plants, each painted a different color. The carvings covered the door from top to bottom and blended into the doorframe. Quin wondered if it would still open, or if the hinges were too rusted and old to work. He unlatched it and then pushed as hard as he could. It creaked and groaned and ever so slowly opened to reveal sunlight on the other side. He turned sideways to squeeze through the opening, letting out his breath to make his large chest as small as possible. Somehow, he still managed to pop two buttons off his shirt. Then he gazed out at the scene in front of him.

A city. Roads, torn up and overwhelmed by grass and weeds. Old buildings, dirty and decrepit from disuse. Homes with collapsed porches and sagging roofs. Trees, branches reaching towards the sky, their leaves quivering in the breeze

He shivered as a sudden gust brushed across his bare head. But he wasn't cold. No, the shiver came from something else. He listened. There were no sounds—no cars, no construction, no laughing or talking, no machines or sirens. It was silent except for the wind. Turning, he looked up at the building he had come out of. A sign hung over his head. It took him a moment to parse out the letters as it was written in old-style Sagittan. It read, "Hemen Temple of Feeling."

Pulling out a piece of paper, he jotted a few things down: *abandoned, piles of dead, Hemen Temple of Feeling, history?* He shook his head. It wasn't his job to figure out what happened here—it was his job to figure out where the Door led. He turned and walked back through the Temple. After all, there was no need to spend much time in an abandoned city if he didn't have to. He had a name and the location was safe enough (unless he suddenly died of a plague); the archaeology team could take it from here.

The Door glittered and sparkled on the dais at the far side of the sanctuary. Quin strode rapidly towards it, trying to ignore how his steps thundered in the echoing room and the way the vibrations made the bones click. He glanced over his shoulder as he walked up the dais steps—hundreds of empty eyes stared at him. Without hesitation, he stepped through the Door and everything went black.

The world around him blurred and fizzled as he reentered the Department of Archeology storage room at the Globe Center. Bin after bin stretched out in front of him, each filled with long cylindrical grey tubes sticking up haphazardly, each one filled with its own closed Door. He sighed and walked over to the computer, rapidly typing a few details about the Door into the system. The computer spat out a small sticker.

Quin turned back to the Door. It rose out of a cylindrical grey tube that sat on the ground in front of him. Quin slapped the sticker on the tube. He would leave the Door open, and then send a message to the archaeology team to come investigate whatever had killed the skeletons in the Hemen Temple of Feeling.

"There you are!" an excited voice called out from the other side of the room. "I've been looking all over for you!"

"I've been stuck in this room for days, more or less," Quin replied without turning his head. John, one of his lifelong friends, worked in the Door Room at the Globe, and had been thrilled when he found out Quin was stationed there for a couple of months.

"What are you doing?" John asked, looking around the dusty room filled with tubes.

"Going through the 'uncategorized' bin," Quin said. "It's what I'm here for."

"Didn't someone just do that?" John asked, frowning. "Seems like it."

"Six years ago," Quin said dryly. "They've confiscated a lot of unregistered Doors since then, apparently."

"So what," John pressed, "you're supposed to find out where they go?"

"That's about right." Quin shrugged and dug through the tubes in the bin. Each tube was thirty-six inches long, and weighed only a few pounds, and the greys varied from bluish to brownish. He had been working through the brownish ones.

"What if you get in trouble?" John asked. "What if something tries to eat you on the other side or the air is poison or you end up in an ocean?"

"If there are any known biological hazards," Quin replied, "such as impure air or an ocean, they automatically get put in the hazard storage. You know that. And the rest—that's why it's my job." He pulled out another brownish grey cylinder, placed it on the ground, and pressed the button on the side. A small humming noise sounded and a Door began to unroll through the top of the cylinder. "So do you need something, or can I get back to work?"

"So we have this Door that I'm working on," John began, sitting down on the edge of a bin. Apparently, he did need something. "And it's shut on the other side."

"And?"

"How do we open it?"

Quin frowned at John. "As far as I know, you can't. Besides, isn't figuring that stuff out your job? Why don't you go do your job and let me do mine?"

"We've tried everything!" John complained, throwing his hands into the air. "We zapped it with different types of radiation, tried sticking things through it—"

"Why do you need to open the Door?" Quin asked.

"We don't, technically. We only need to find the other side. If we know where it is, we can go get it."

Quin thought for a moment. The Doors were stored in tubes—as far as he knew, that was the only way to keep one shut. He picked up one of the cylinders. "So, if the other side is most likely stored in a tube," he said, "maybe all you need to do is make a tracking device that is small enough to fit inside the tube. You could push it through with your hand."

John's eyes widened. "We haven't tried that yet!"

Quin nodded. Maybe John would go away now.

Instead, he sat there, musing and muttering to himself. "It would have to go through long enough for us to get a signal, maybe a little longer—I would have to build something really thin because I think all we have are…"

Quin cleared his throat. "Can I get back to work?"

"No!" John exclaimed, his attention suddenly shifting back to Quin. He reached up to straighten his brightly-colored tie and frowned. "Speaking of gambling, I hear you had drinks with Mavis Oliphant last night."

"We weren't talking about gambling," Quin grumbled. John's non-sequiturs drove him crazy, especially when they involved talking about his own personal business.

"Yes, we were," John said. "The Door I'm working on was confiscated when the police busted up an illegal gambling ring."

"I see," Quin said. "And how was I supposed to know that?"

John ignored his question. "So is it true?"

"What?"

"Did you get drinks with Mavis Oliphant?"

"I didn't have drinks, just saw her while I was out."

"She's bad news, Quin," John said. "You watch out, okay?"

"She's an old lady," Quin argued, annoyed. John was always meddling in Quin's life. It was none of his business! "But fine. Whatever you say. I'm getting back to work now. I still have eight hundred more Doors to go through." He rolled open another Door and reset the hover cam.

"Can I come?" John asked eagerly, his face once again an excited smile.

"No," Quin replied. He reset the hover cam and pushed it through the Door in front of him. Then he picked up his walking stick

"But you can't really stop me."

"No," Quin said again. "But you're wearing the wrong kind of shoes for this." He gestured to his own boots, with reinforced toes and a thick hide that would protect him against most types of problems. He also wore a heavy jacket, in case of cold, and a backpack with water and food, in case he got lost or had trouble getting back to the Door for any reason.

John wore high-quality dress shoes, designed for walking around in office buildings and a tie patterned with dinosaurs.

"I think I'll risk it," he replied cheerily, grinning at Quin.

Quin shrugged. Let John's supervisor deal with him. He shoulder his backpack, stepped through the Door—

—and landed with a splash. He stood in the middle of a hot, humid swamp. Flies buzzed around his head and the smell of swamp gases filled the air. The trees had silvery-green leaves, and the grasses were so sharp they sliced at his pant legs.

"Oh no!" he heard from behind him. John was hopping around and shrieking, "My feet! My feet!" as loudly as he could muster. "They're wet!"

Quin chuckled to himself and turned to see John disappear back through the Door.

CHAPTER 2

"Would you stop maiming my boyfriends?" Jo exclaimed, storming into the house. Rainwater poured from her head and jacket, pooling under her feet. She tossed the jacket across a short bannister between two columns and stomped across the marble floor into the drawing room where she knew her father, Nash, would be reading.

"What are you talking about?" he asked, setting down his book and looking at her with an innocent expression. Nash mostly read the newspaper, but when he picked up a book, it was usually on finance or economics. He would underline sentences and do little equations in the margins, and fold down the corners of pages he wanted to find easily again.

"You heard me, Nash!" Jo put her hands on her hips, glaring at her father. She always called him by his first name, because she knew it annoyed him. "Troy is in the hospital with two broken legs and a broken finger, and I know it was you! That's the third time in one year! At this rate, no one will ever date me for fear of losing an eye! And yes, he broke up with me, in case you were wondering."

"Well, I should hope so," Nash said, sitting back in his chair. There was a reason people called him Nasty Nash, and he knew it. He did what he wanted, said what he wanted, and took what he wanted. "You're a disgrace! Can't even pick a lock properly. Besides, if you quit dating men who owe me money, they might not get into so many… accidents." A small smile played on his lips and she knew he was manipulating her—to do what, she wasn't sure, but she recognized the feeling and it burned.

She could feel rage building up, red hot. Every single day she woke up knowing she could be arrested for things her father had done, or that she could get caught in the middle of something worse than petty theft, or that she would come home to a house full of hookers, gamblers, or worse—police! All she wanted was to live a normal, legal life. She took a deep breath and put a neutral expression on her face. It wouldn't do for Nash to know how much affect he had on her.

"Let me know when you've decided on a more lucrative career than garden center employee—" Nash let out a snort, "and then we can talk."

"I'm a horticulturalist!" she hollered back, and stormed up the stairs and into her room.

It was time, she decided as she toweled off her hair and shed her soaking wet clothes. She was moving out, no matter what Nash said. Hopefully he wouldn't burn her apartment to the ground, but she at least had to make the effort. A new house, her own stuff, her own schedule, her own boyfriends.

"Oh, honey," her dad called up the stairs. "Look nice tonight, why don't you? I'm having some friends over."

She growled under her breath and pulled open her closet, stepping inside. It was the last time. Tomorrow, she'd be out.

✳✳✳✳✳

"Sorry to hear about Troy, sweetie," Carl called as Jo delivered drinks to his table. She scowled at him and headed back towards the kitchen. She really needed to get it together. It was fine to be angry with her father, but she shouldn't take it out on other people. She took a deep breath and put a smile on her face, taking a few extra seconds to make sure it reached to the lines around her eyes.

Her father had outdone himself tonight. It was the first time in months he had hosted a night of "friendly games," as he called it, and over a hundred people had shown up. She would serve drinks until midnight, and then switch to the Rabbit's Foot table—hopefully after all of the potential tags had left for the night. Rabbit's Foot was a highly illegal game that sometimes ended in death, and she wished her father would stop hosting it. On the other hand, she was an excellent and distracting dealer, which her father paid her to do. She could make enough money tonight to pay a month's rent several times over—and as long as she wore her body armor, she wouldn't die.

"Can't seem to keep 'em!" Chuck yelled as she strolled by, reaching out to pinch her. "Don't worry baby, you always got me."

She scowled at him briefly, making a mental note to spill his beer all over his lap the next time she stopped at his table, and then put her smile back on. The room was filled with raucous laughter and angry exclamations; card games happened on nearly every table, with her dad's most trusted associates dealing at the large tables in the center of the room.

At 11:00 she set down her drinks. She had to start getting sign-ups for Rabbit's Foot.

"Stanky," she yelled into the kitchen. His actual name was Stevie, but everyone who worked with him preferred Stanky, mostly because he always smelled like he left his laundry in the washing machine a few days too many. "I'm going to go get names! Get Sylvia to cover me!"

"Got it!" Stanky called back, grinning and giving her the thumbs up. Out of all the people who worked with or for her dad, she thought she probably liked Stanky the best.

Heading back out to the main room, she picked the closest table—where Matty and Matt played their own random game of dice and chance, and climbed up on top of it so she could see the whole room. She gave a piercing whistle and the room quieted almost immediately.

"SIGN-UPS, THAT CORNER!" she yelled pointing to the corner on the opposite side of the room. She hopped down from the table as the room filled back up with noise. "Thanks guys," she said, smiling at Matty and Matt.

The first three sign-ups were guys she had known since she had first started running games for her father in high school. Old farts, as she thought of them, who needed a little danger in their lives. They had played many times over the years, and even had a few scars to show for it. She thought they were nuts, but clearly they had too much money and not enough to do.

Next up was Mavis. She was so old Jo thought she could probably die at any minute. None of her family paid any attention to her, and she didn't really have any friends. She had been a musician in her younger days—albeit a rather unsuccessful one. But even though she owed mountains of debt to Jo's father, Nash let Mavis keep playing because he felt sorry for her.

"You're too old for this game," Jo said. She glanced over at Nash who stood next to a far wall. He gave her a thumbs-up and pointed to a bag he held over his shoulder, and then to Mavis. She must have paid off some or all of her debt.

"If I die," Mavis argued, adjusting the collar on her yellow flowered dress, "then I won't owe any more money to your dad."

"How much do you still owe?"

"Nothing," Mavis said, smiling through her wrinkles. "I paid him. You can go ask!"

Jo shook her head and rolled her eyes. "If you say so," she said, and wrote her name on the list.

"I'm in," said a young man in a suit, looking around nervously. He wore glasses and carried a briefcase. On the surface, he looked like a young businessman who was only there to try his luck, but Jo had a weird feeling about him. She frowned.

"Who's your sponsor?

"Chuck DeLaney."

Chuck was one of those people who always said, "Sure, I know that guy!" whether he actually did or not. Not a reliable sponsor, to say the least.

"You know what you're in for?" she asked.

"Yeah, yeah," he said, looking around nervously again. He leaned in and whispered, "Is it Rabbit's Foot?"

Jo frowned and began to observe a little more carefully. The jacket he wore didn't fit quite right, and he was rubbing his right forefinger with his thumb. His shoes had mud on them, and his hair was a mess. He was dressed like he thought he should be, not like a normal person. Besides, anyone who knew what they were talking about would have answered her question with a number, not asked which game it was. You either knew—or you didn't.

"What's that on your collar?" she asked, pointing to his shirt.

"Oh, what? This?" he said, looking down, brushing his collar gently. "Just, you know, a hair or something."

"Why do they always send in the worst of you lot?" she asked, sighing. She raised her right hand in a fist, and in less than five seconds, two large bouncers appeared, each grabbing one of the man's arms.

"Mole," she said, crossing her arms. "Get him out of here."

"Need any help?" said the next man in line. He was tall with broad shoulders and a shiny bald head. His suit fit perfectly, except that where his muscles bulged, the seams appeared to be crying out in agony.

"Who are you?" she asked, scowling at him. This had better not be some elaborate trick—get one mole dragged out and put another right in line behind him.

"Name's Quin Black," he said. "I'd like to sign up."

"Who's your sponsor?"

The man gestured over his shoulder. "Mavis Oliphant," he replied.

"She doesn't have friends."

"Didn't say we were friends."

She paused, staring at the newcomer. It was always a risk with the newbies. "What're you in for?" she asked, still frowning.

"Ten thousand," he replied.

She raised her eyebrows and held out her tablet. "Sign." They didn't really use the signature for anything, but it made the agreement seem more official, and often made newcomers feel nervous. This guy didn't seem nervous though. He nodded and held out his finger, scribbling a nearly illegible name.

"First round," she said, writing his name on her list, "you're up."

By the time midnight rolled around, she had gotten thirty people to sign up—enough for three rounds. It was a good number—not a record, by any means, but enough to make a significant amount of money that night. She smiled. She should get enough to put a deposit down on an apartment.

She slipped into her body armor—it wasn't uncommon for people to die playing this game—and strolled over to the Rabbit's Foot table, taking her position in the middle. The three old white guys sat next to the bald black guy and tried to talk to him, but he ignored them. Mavis sat on his other side, but Quin didn't talk to her either. He was sitting perfectly still, his chips on the table in front of him. The other five people at the table—two black women, a man with blue pointed ears that made him look like he was from the planet Pantal, and an androgynous person chatted pleasantly with each other.

"You all understand how this game works?" she asked. Everyone quieted down immediately and nodded but she continued with her normal speech anyway. "You need a run of cards of the same species." The cards had animals on them—players could get a run of fish, mammals, insects, or birds. "You bid at each round, or you drop out and are obligated to pay what you bid in the beginning. If you get a run, you are required to battle with the White Rabbit—me. If you beat me, you win the pot. If I beat you, I win the money."

Everyone was nodding as if that was exactly what they had expected—except for Quin. He sat perfectly still, looking straight ahead. Mavis had a little smile on her face. She enjoyed this far too much—especially given that she was probably going to lose. Again.

"Please take two cards," she said, spinning in a circle again, rapidly offering cards to each of the ten people who sat at the table.

Black looked at his cards briefly and then set them on the table in front of him. He was watching the faces of the other people around them. That was smart, she thought. If someone got a

16

matching pair, he would know and could make decisions based on probabilities. Nash didn't like it when people paid attention, but since it was nearly impossible to count cards in this game, he didn't get too up and arms over it, unless someone won over and over again. Then he might give a simple warning—a broken finger or arm most likely. Though, this Quin guy didn't seem like the type to let someone break his finger.

She waited another minute and then held out a bucket. "If you'd like to see the Rabbit's cards," she intoned, "please place a token in the bucket."

Everyone in the circle placed a token in the bucket. That was good. People who bailed out early made Nash mad. He preferred to suck up as much money from these people as possible.

She laid two new cards on the table.

"Fiddlesticks!" one of the old men exclaimed. "I'm out already, what do you know?" His friends ribbed and harassed him as he threw down his cards and stalked off. The new guy didn't move—his face didn't even twitch. After a moment, though, she noticed his eyes flick to the cards the old man had thrown down. He was definitely keeping track.

She spun the bucket around again and showed the next card.

"I'm all in," Quin said, but three others dropped out.

She was about to spin the bucket around again when she heard a commotion on the other side of the room. Stanky had come out of the kitchen, which was generally not allowed, but he looked nervous, twitchy, and kept pointing and shouting towards the kitchen.

Finally, he yelled at the top of his lungs, "FIRE!"

Gasping, Jo stood up in the middle of the table, about to jump down, when the kitchen erupted in a huge ball of flame. A wave of heat washed over her followed by a brain-rattling wall of sound. The next moment, she was flying backwards through the air, and all she could think about was that it smelled like tacos. Then everything went dark.

CHAPTER 3

Quin was under the table before he even knew what he was doing. The explosion reverberated through the building, followed by a series of small popping noises. Everyone in the room ran towards the main entrance, screaming, trying to get out. A few people who had been near the kitchen lay unmoving on the floor or draped across chairs.

Quin waited a moment to see if any more explosions would come and then crawled out from under the table, slowly and cautiously picking his way towards an exit. He didn't want to be here when the cops arrived. Though he probably wouldn't be arrested, he would definitely be questioned since he worked for the government, and his supervisor would be alerted—and it might possibly ruin his career.

He noticed that Mavis had fallen out of her chair, but was now crawling slowly towards the exit. He moved to go help her but before he got very close, another person leaned down, grabbed the old woman's arm, and led her towards the main exit. The main entrance was clogged by people climbing over each other, pulling hair, and scratching, so Quin decided to try to find an alternate exit. As he moved across the room, he noticed that the White Rabbit was lying unconscious on the ground, black braids spreading in all directions from her head. He knelt to check her pulse—still alive.

She groaned and moved her head.

Quin glanced back at the door where so many people were trying to escape. He could leave her here, and probably should, but she would most definitely get arrested since she was running the

White Rabbit game. He could also get her out and give her a chance to escape. She wasn't very old—going to jail would be a rough way to start life. He shrugged and bent down, lifting her into his arms while trying to support her neck. She was small-boned, but muscled.

He headed towards a side door. It was locked. He set her down, and then slammed his shoulder against it. It broke open. He leaned down, picked up the White Rabbit again, and stepped into a hallway. The door on the one end was unlocked; the lobby on the other side boasted tall columns and a winding staircase. Quin rushed forward to the exit and peered out into the street. No emergency vehicles had arrived yet, so he slipped out and headed down the street, quickly ducking into the first alley he came across. He would look quite suspicious wandering down the street carrying an unconscious girl.

What should he do? He hadn't brought any form of communication or identification with him because he didn't want to risk being caught, or his wallet getting lifted, or anyone being able to track him to the location. But he couldn't leave a woman lying on the street, unconscious. He had to get her somewhere safe, but without being seen. He thought for a moment. There was a convenience store at the end of the street. It might have a phone. He could call John or Pete, who could come get them both, and take them somewhere safe. After another second of thought, he decided to leave John out of it. He was too erratic—plus he was under obligation to report any illegal doings of his colleagues to the directors at the Globe.

Quin arranged the woman so she was lying semi-comfortably and out of sight from any casual passersby, and then strode calmly and confidently down the street. He didn't want it to appear that he had anything to do with the commotion.

The bell dinged as he strode into the convenience shop. The fluorescent lights flickered annoyingly, and the shelves were filled with a colorful array of largely inedible snacks. The guy behind the counter was sitting back, reading a magazine, and chewing on a piece of jerky. He glanced out the window every time he heard a siren or the lights of another emergency vehicle flashed through the window.

"Hey," Quin said.

"Evening," the cashier replied. "You know what's going on out there?"

"Some kind of explosion," Quin replied casually, shrugging as if that was all he knew. "Could I borrow a phone?"

The guy pointed at a public use phone hanging on the wall. "No problem, man. Costs ten cents per minute."

"Thanks." He picked up the phone and looked at it for a moment, imagining all the filthy ears that had probably touched it. It didn't matter, though—he dialed Pete collect.

"Who is this?" Pete asked as he picked up. He didn't like getting calls from unknown numbers.

"Me. I need a ride." Quin gave the address and hung up.

"Must've been a big explosion," the cashier said as another ambulance went by.

"Don't know much about it," Quin said, shrugging again. He gave a wave, "Thanks," and headed out the door.

The White Rabbit was still unconscious when he got back to the alley. He waited in the shadows until Pete's car pulled up. Instead of a typical hover vehicle, Pete drove an old Earthan Ford that he had picked up from some unusual items dealer. It ran on petroleum, and smelled awful, but he liked it for some reason.

Quin carefully lifted the woman and slid her into Pete's backseat, climbing into the front himself.

"What have you gotten yourself into?" Pete asked, scowling. Quin had known Pete for a long time, ever since they were kids. They had done all kinds of crazy (and sometimes illegal) things together, but Pete had a solid moral line, and kidnapping people definitely crossed it.

"Take me to Dad's house," Quin said. He didn't want to tell Pete too much—didn't want him to know that he had gotten back into gambling if he could avoid it.

"You have something to do with all this commotion?" Pete asked.

Quin remained silent.

"I'm not taking you anywhere until you tell me what's going on," Pete said. "I'll even go so far as to call one of these cops over and tell him you loaded an unconscious woman into my back seat."

"Okay, okay," Quin growled. This was taking too long and Pete's car was nothing if not noticeable. "I'll tell you. Just get out of here, please."

Pete pulled away from the curb and turned on the first street that led in the opposite direction of the firetrucks and police cars.

"Talk," Pete ordered.

The one thing Quin knew about Pete was that he could keep his silence, though he would still probably lecture Quin about choices.

"I was gambling," Quin said. "And there was an explosion."

"Who's the girl?"

"She was the White Rabbit. Got flung off the table in the explosion and hit her head."

"You were playing White Rabbit?" Pete exclaimed, shaking his head. "You're an idiot, you know that?"

Quin shrugged. "I can usually win if I get a good set of cards."

"Yeah," Pete said, "I can see—you obviously haven't died yet. Not for lack of trying. You shouldn't take her back to your house though."

"What do you suggest?" Quin asked.

A few minutes later they pulled up in front of Pete's Clocks, a business Pete had inherited from his father, also named Pete.

"Here?" Quin asked, frowning. "Won't people notice you dragging in an unconscious girl in the middle of the night?"

"Nah," he replied, pulling down the alley between his building and the store next door. "We'll take her through the back door. And Les is here, so she can make sure White Rabbit is okay."

Pete led him in the back door. Quin had been in this room many times, and when Pete flicked the lights on, it looked no different than

21

he remembered. Three old couches with hideously colored patterns sat against the walls. A mini-kitchen with a small fridge and sink took up one corner. Some filing cabinets stuffed to overflowing with papers had been pushed up against the wall, and a staircase led up to the second floor from one corner.

"Les!" Pete yelled up the stairs as Quin laid the White Rabbit on the couch. "Got an unconscious woman down here!"

"Coming!" Leslie bounded down the stairs in her pajamas and knelt by the unconscious girl, poking and prodding and checking for vitals. She and Pete had been married for two years or so, and were the happiest couple Quin thought he had ever met. Leslie was a multi-species neurosurgeon, and Pete sold clocks while also running an interplanetary network of political informants.

"Seems fine," Leslie proclaimed after a minute. "Just unconscious. Give her some time to wake up."

"Good," Pete said, turning to Quin. "Now, do you want to tell me what the bumbleswats you think you were doing? Gambling? At Nasty Nash's?"

"Oooh was it busy?" Leslie asked, grinning. She pulled back her dark hair into a ponytail, and raised her eyebrows at Quin. "Did you see anybody you knew?"

"Les," Pete scolded. "We shouldn't be encouraging him."

Leslie laughed and elbowed Pete. "But I've always wanted to go! I'm so curious!"

"He was playing White Rabbit," Pete added.

"Dangerous game." Leslie's voice suddenly switched to stern. "And also very illegal! Quin, what were you thinking?"

Quin rolled his eyes. These two worried, but there was nothing to worry about. He always won White Rabbit—all you had to do was stick with it until the end, and not get stupid cards. It wasn't that hard.

Then the door burst open. Quin leaped to his feet, ready for an attack.

"What on earth were you thinking, Quin Black?" John demanded, his hands on his hips. "You are quite stupid for someone who is reasonably intelligent!"

Quin relaxed and sat back down. It was only John. Of course, him being here was nearly as bothersome as if the police had showed up. Now that he knew Quin had gotten back into his gambling habit, he would nag and poke and prod without end. But Quin knew he had already been suspicious—it had only been a matter of time until he found out.

"What are you doing here?" Quin asked.

"Finding out what trouble you've been causing, that's what," John replied. "I thought you gave up gambling! I thought you were clean! What do you think you're doing, getting back into it again? I'm not going to bail you out this time, you know. I'm not. You're on your own." He paused suddenly, noting the woman on the couch. "And you've got Nasty Nash's daughter unconscious on the couch?" He dramatically grabbed his face with his hands and looked woefully at the ceiling. "What have you gotten yourself into?"

"Nasty Nash's daughter?" Pete repeated, looking at her sleeping from. "Well. That could be a problem."

Quin shrugged. "Could be. Or not."

"How could it *not* be a problem?" John demanded. "She's UNCONSCIOUS. ON YOUR COUCH."

"It's Pete's couch, to be fair," Quin replied.

"Yeah, maybe we should take her to your place after all," Pete said. "Nasty Nash isn't the type I like to get involved with."

"Oh hush, all of you," Leslie interrupted. "Quin did a nice thing, rescuing her from an explosion like that. When she wakes up, we'll explain what happened and send her on her way."

"Explain what?" asked a soft voice.

Quin shifted his attention abruptly towards the couch. Nasty Nash's daughter sat there frowning, looking up at the others in the room.

"Where am I?" Her frown deepened as she reached up to touch her head.

"Safe," Leslie said, kneeling next to the couch. "You hit your head and have been unconscious. We were trying to make sure you woke up safely."

The look of suspicion on her face wasn't going away. "Who are you people?" Then her eyes lit on Quin. "I know you! You were..." She paused as if she were trying very hard to remember. "...at my table! That's it—you were at Dad's thing there, the gambling night. How did I get here?"

"There was an explosion," Quin replied. "Cops were coming, and you were unconscious so I dragged you out."

"Why didn't you let me get arrested?" she asked, her voice still highly suspicious. She reached up hesitantly to touch a scratch on her dark cheekbone.

Quin shrugged. "It didn't seem fair. Everyone else could run, you couldn't. Plus you were in the way. It was easier to drag you out than jump over you."

She sat up slowly. "So, I'm free to go?"

"Of course," Quin replied, gesturing towards the door. "The explosion was only a few hours ago, so there will likely be emergency vehicles still around the building." He waved. "Have a nice evening."

She stood slowly and took a few stumbling steps towards the door, where she grabbed onto the doorframe for balance.

"Is your head okay?" Leslie asked. "I'm a doctor—if you need anything, give me a call."

Nasty Nash's daughter nodded. "Okay, whoever you are. Thanks for rescuing me, I think." She took a few steps forward, as if she were testing her sense of balance, and then strode towards the door. "Bye."

The door swung shut behind her.

"Time for some shut-eye," Quin said, yawning and stretching.

"Harumph," John said.

"That's not actually a word," Quin remarked.

"I am not through with you," John said, crossing his arms. "We are going to have some serious chats, and you are going back to counseling."

"Probably a good idea," Pete agreed.

"I know a great one, if you'd like a new one," Leslie offered.

"Yeah, sure, thanks guys," Quin said. He wasn't going to counseling, he knew that. The last three counselors he saw had been disasters in people suits. One had him writing down his feelings daily—what feelings? *The air feels warm today?*—and another wanted him to elaborate on his mother's death *every single week*. That got old fast. The last one wasn't too bad, but her sense of logic didn't match up to Quin's and he found himself a little confused every time he went to see her. She had also kept pushing him to try hypnotism, and that was something Quin was definitely not interested in.

He stood, and yawned again. "I'll catch a cab back to my place. See you later."

Then he stepped out into the warm Pomegranate City night.

CHAPTER 4

Jo walked as quickly as she could away from the strange clock-shaped building she had woken up in, but it was difficult as her head hurt and she felt a little dizzy. She stumbled a few times as she walked, but the cold air helped her think more clearly. The people seemed nice enough, and she supposed she should be grateful that this Quin Black person had rescued her, but the whole thing was very odd. And if her dad's house really had blown up, who was responsible? And was her dad even alive?

Her breath came in shorter gasps as she hurried through the streets. She could see red and blue lights flashing ahead, and when she was only one block away, she ducked into an alley. She needed a plan. She needed to know—was her dad still alive? What about Stanky or Sylvia? There were so many people she knew and even partially cared about! And if she could get inside, she could get her stash of cash, which would allow her to disappear.

She was still wearing the body armor from being White Rabbit, but the clothes she had on over top of it were clean and untorn. She didn't look as if she had been in an explosion—as far as she could tell. She could probably walk up to the cop, pretending to be distraught and asking for survivors, and the police would feel sorry for her and tell her what she wanted to know.

Jo just hoped she could be convincing.

She took a deep breath and put on her worried face, angling her eyebrows so they made wrinkles over her nose, and worked up some alligator tears. Then she stepped out of the alley, striding right up to the police tape that blocked off the end of the street.

"Excuse me!" she called out. "Officer? Officer!" She waved her hand and then patted her throat, like she was so stressed she was having trouble breathing.

"I'm sorry, ma'am," a police officer stated, "but this is an emergency scene. We can't let you inside the perimeter."

"But this is my house!" She tried to make her voice sound overwrought and stressed. She had to make them believe she had no idea why the police were there. She had to make them believe she was completely innocent. "What happened? Where's my dad? Is he okay?"

"What's your name?" the officer asked.

"Jo," she replied. "Jo Nash. Where's my dad?" She really was almost crying now. It hadn't really made a full impact on her that her dad could be dead—or worse, missing—until this very moment. She might not like him very much, but she did care.

"Please, come this way," the police officer said, holding up the tape for her to step under. "Your father is injured, but he'll be fine. He's on his way to the hospital. I'm Officer Reynolds and I can take you there, but I'll need to ask you a few questions first."

"Okay, sure, fine," Jo replied. "But make it quick, please. I need to go inside."

"I'm sorry," Officer Reynolds said. "You can't go inside. The emergency personnel are still checking for remains, and the building is unsound. You will have to wait until tomorrow."

Purple binnow rats, Jo thought. She had to wait until tomorrow *and* now she had to talk to the police until they were done with her. Talk about a bad call on her part. The worry she had for her father dissipated immediately, and she shifted her focus onto maintaining her façade of concern.

The next half hour was a blur. Police officers asked her dozens of questions about what had been going on in the house when the explosion occurred. She told them the story that she and Nash had agreed on years ago—a house party, nothing more and nothing less—with a few of Nash's colleagues. Then she added her own details—she had been there but went to meet up with a friend, and returned in a hurry when she heard there was an explosion, and could she please see her father now because she was very worried about him and wanted to make sure he was okay.

"One more question," Officer Reynolds said. "Could you please tell us the name of the friend you were visiting? For an alibi, you understand."

Jo mentally berated herself for not saying she had gone out to run errands or something else that would not have an alibi. She couldn't trust Quin Black and his friends, could she? But what other choice did she have? Quin would have to confirm her alibi—otherwise, he would have to admit to being at a house party thrown by Nasty Nash. That couldn't be good for his career. But maybe there was something she could do first. Maybe she could distract the officer from the question by becoming upset.

"You don't think I have something to do with this, do you?" She tried to sound offended, though she worried that her voice was too high-pitched and it might have come across as nervous instead.

"We don't know yet," the officer began, but Jo cut her off.

"What a horrible thing to say to a person whose father has just been in a terrible accident and is on his way to the hospital! You could at very least take me there and ask me all of these terrible questions later. I want to see my father!" She realized as she was saying this that she didn't really want to see her father at all, that just knowing he was alive was more than enough information for her. But if he was her only way to get out of this, then she would use it. "I'm tired and stressed and upset, and now here you are accusing ME of trying to blow up my own house! It's uncalled for, rude, and extremely upsetting."

Officer Reynolds began again. "I understand that, but—"

"Do you understand? *Do you?*" Jo raised her voice as loudly as she could without screaming. "Have you ever come home to find your home in flames because of an EXPLOSION and heard that your father was injured and on the way to the hospital only to have the police tell you they think you're responsible—"

"*He had an insurance policy,*" Officer Reynolds said loudly, cutting Jo off. "On himself, for several million dollars. There is plenty of motive right there, if you ask me or any other police officer. Now if you would please calm down and cooperate for two more minutes, then we will take you to your father. Please tell me the name of your alibi."

Damn. It didn't work. Obviously nothing was going to make Officer Reynolds forget about the alibi question and let her go.

"A name." Officer Reynolds stared Jo down. "Unless you don't have one? It was all a lie?"

Jo sighed and mumbled barely loudly enough for the police officer to hear, "Quin Black."

"What did you say?"

"Quin Black," she said a little more loudly.

"Did I hear you say Quin Black?" Officer Reynolds asked, her eyebrows so far up her head they could have been mistaken for hair.

"Yes," Jo mumbled.

"Well, then," Officer Reynolds quickly sent a message to someone. "He is an extremely reliable source of information. I don't know why you didn't just tell me that right off. Shall we be going then?"

*****

The hospital smelled like a noxious blend of antiseptic and lemon juice, and the clean walls and floor looked as though they had recently been scrubbed. Officer Reynolds dropped her off at the front entrance of the hospital, and Jo decided she should go to the desk to ask about her father. She had thought about sneaking out the back and trying to avoid this entire conversation, but she had a feeling she was being watched, and decided she should at least put on a good show, no matter how tired or annoyed she was.

She carefully arranged her face into that of a worried daughter and rushed up to the nurse at the front desk.

"I'm looking for my father," she said rapidly. "He was in an explosion and the police told me he was brought here and I need to see him to make sure he's okay."

"Last name Nash?" the nurse confirmed. "He's in Room 32, and I believe he just woke up."

"Oh thank you, thank you so much! You are really wonderful!" Jo gushed and rushed down the hall towards room 32.

Another nurse was attending him when she arrived.

"Oh, Dad!" she exclaimed, for the benefit of the nurse. "I'm so glad you're okay! I was so worried! And when I heard from a friend that there was an explosion, I left and came back immediately." She leaned down to give him a hug, and then asked, "What happened to your face?" He had a long bloody scar that ran across his forehead.

He nodded, clearly understanding that she had somehow left the house and come back.

"I'm glad you weren't there, dear," he said hoarsely.

"He's going to be fine," the nurse said. "A mild concussion, a cut where he hit his head, and some contusions, but nothing that shouldn't heal up in the next week or so."

"Oh thank you, thank you!" Jo waited until the nurse left the room and then turned back to her father. "What happened?" she hissed. "What are they going to find?"

"Not much," her dad replied. "Jonas did his job well, and hid everything that would indicate anything illegal. Not sure what caused the explosion. I told them it was nothing more than a card game with friends. I've got Mason looking into it."

"Mason," Jo scoffed. "She's completely incompetent."

"Well, you're welcome to dig around if you think you can do a better job," Nash said harshly. "Just check with her first to see if she's learned anything. What happened to you anyway?"

"I got knocked out and somebody dragged me to safety," she replied. "But as far as you know, I was out visiting a friend."

"Oh? What friend?" he asked.

"None of your business." She crossed her arms. "Daughters don't tell their dads everything after all."

"Fine," he said. He gestured to his bag. "There's some cash there—take it so the cops don't find it. They haven't searched me yet. Too focused on getting me here. Oh, and those three cylinders in there—they should go too. Take the whole bag."

"What are they?" she asked curiously.

"Payment of a debt," he replied. "But they're illegal so get them out of here before the cops find out I'm awake."

She bent down and dug through the bag, quickly stuffing the cash into her pockets and bra. It wasn't a huge amount of money, but enough to make someone suspicious. She would make it disappear. Maybe even use it for a deposit on an apartment.

She left the three cylinders in the bag and slung it over her shoulder—they were heavier than she expected. She'd drop them off at Mason's when she stopped by—let her deal with her dad's crap.

"I'm going to go now," she said.

"Let me know if you find anything out," Nash replied, coughing a little into his hand, "and I'll show them they're messing with the wrong guy!"

Jo took the back way out of the hospital, to avoid running into or being followed by Officer Reynolds. She walked down back alleys and side paths through the city until she arrived at Mason's house. Jo and Mason had never gotten along, at least not since Mason had started dating Nash. Meg Mason had been a basic pickpocket and scam artist when she had tried to snag Nash's wallet on the street one day. Instead of kicking her out of his territory, he had taken her in—all the way in. Jo found Mason to be snide and annoying, and the fact that she was around all the time was another really good reason for Jo to disappear for good.

"You find anything yet?" she asked, bursting in through the door without knocking. Mason sat in the kitchen with three of her buddies. They were discussing tactics.

"Oh hello, sweetheart," Mason said. Her voice grated on Jo's nerves. "So glad you're okay. Your dad was worried about you."

"I'm sure," Jo replied. "Where were you?" She dropped the cylinders wrapped in her dad's coat on the table. She figured she could leave them there—let Mason deal with them.

"On the other side of the house," she replied. "Close enough to be of help, but not close enough to get injured."

"Very convenient, I'm sure," Jo muttered. "Have you figured out anything about who might have done it?"

"We have a list of names of people who were in the kitchen before and after the explosion. We eliminated the dead ones—because why, after all?—and have three names remaining." She gestured to her friends. "Jace and Camile here will interrogate them, while Jorge and I will go collecting."

"Collecting?" It seemed like a strange thing to do when someone was clearly trying to kill her father. Weren't there more important things to be doing? Like finding the bomber?

"Of course," Mason said. "We will need money to rebuild, after all."

"Dad know about this?"

"Of course—it was his idea." Mason smiled a little, and Jo scowled back. The smile always unnerved her—lips too thin, eyes too narrow, brows too low, like she knew something that Jo didn't and it pleased her.

"Who's on your list?" Jo asked.

"That is none of your concern."

"Fine. Whatever." Jo turned to leave.

"Oh, and Jo," Mason said.

Jo paused and turned to look back.

"Be careful out there. Whoever wants your dad dead might want you dead too." There it was, that smile again. That was a threat if she'd ever heard one.

Jo shook her head once. "I'll be fine," she said, and stormed out the door. She was going to have to keep a closer eye on Mason.

32

As soon as she left Mason's, Jo realized something: she had nowhere to go. Her house had been demolished, she didn't trust Mason, and her dad was in the hospital. She was exhausted and needed a place to sleep for at least a few hours, so she wandered up to a motel not too far away from the hospital and checked in. The clerk gave her a funny look—after all, she had no luggage or purse and she had pulled a wad of cash out of her pocket—but then showed her to her room and left her alone.

She slept late into the morning, despite the fact that the bed was extremely uncomfortable and itchy. The hotel offered a complimentary breakfast, which she scarfed up only minutes before they closed the kitchen for the morning.

When she exited the hotel, once again she felt lost. Where was she supposed to go? What was she supposed to do? She didn't have class for another two days, since her father only let her take classes on a part-time basis. Her house was still destroyed, and what few friends she had who hadn't been maimed because they owed her father money would be working. She should vanish, but to do that, she would need more resources than she currently had. She needed to get back into the house.

She began to wander aimlessly, and before long ended up standing in front of the hospital.

Officer Reynolds was parked out front. Jo tried to turn around and head back in the direction she had come from, but it was too late. Officer Reynolds was waving her down.

"Good morning!" she said. "I hope you had a good night's sleep."

"I did, thanks," Jo replied politely. She decided to put on a sort of sad and depressed look, hoping that Officer Reynolds would feel sorry for her and leave her alone.

"I wanted to follow up on you this morning," Officer Reynolds said. "We have some new evidence in the explosion—we think we might know where the explosives came from."

"Yeah?" Jo asked. "Where?"

"A local hardware store called *Bricks and Flicks*. They rent movies too."

"Interesting," Jo said, keeping her face politely neutral. Her uncle owned *Bricks and Flicks*. She wondered if the police had figured that out, too.

"And we found a long, brown hair inside one of the components of the device that was flung out as the bomb detonated."

"It was an actual bomb?" Jo asked. "Not a gas leak or something?"

"It appears to have been an actual bomb, yes," Officer Reynolds.

Jo frowned. Mason had long brown hair. But why would she try to blow up Nash? Jo brushed off the thought. A lot of people had long brown hair.

"Can you think of any connections between your father and *Bricks and Flicks*?" Officer Reynolds asked.

"Um, yeah," Jo said. She knew they would figure out the connection eventually anyway—there was no need for her to get in trouble for not being forthcoming on this particular question. "My uncle owns it. But I'm pretty sure he didn't blow us up."

"Interesting," Officer Reynolds said, making a note.

"I'm sorry," Jo said, feigning more tiredness than she felt. "But I would really like to go see my dad now, is that okay?"

"Of course," Officer Reynolds said, waving Jo towards the building. "I'm sorry to bother you. We will be in touch if we have any more questions. Thank you so much!"

"Of course," Jo said, and once again she found herself wandering into a hospital that she had no interest in being in. She began to devise a plan to sneak out the back, but was surprised to see her father talking to a nurse in the lobby, face wrapped in bandages.

"Jo!" he exclaimed. "So glad to see you. I was just checking myself out."

"Have the doctors given you permission to leave?" Jo asked.

"Absolutely," he replied smiling. "And it's so wonderful of you to come help me get home."

"Uh, sure," Jo said, putting a smile on her face so it looked to the nurse like Jo was thrilled her father was getting out of the hospital early. "Officer Reynolds is outside," she said, "if you want to ask her anything."

"Oh, no," Nash said. "Let's head out the back door, why don't we?"

Jo stepped forward, smiling pleasantly at the nurse, and helped her father walk casually out the back door of the hospital. As soon as they were outside, Jo dropped his arm.

"Well," she said, "I'll see you later then."

"Hang on a second," Nash said, reaching out to grab her wrist. "Why'd you come by the hospital?"

"I was trying to avoid Officer Reynolds," Jo said. "I didn't realize you would be up—I wasn't even going to come see you."

"But you still wandered by the hospital," Nash argued. "Aimlessly, I suspect?" He smiled when she crossed her arms and remained silent. "Because you don't know where to go."

She still didn't speak.

"Look," Nash said. "I know you want to go to school, so how about I make you a deal? I'll pay your college tuition—full semesters for an entire degree—if you help me with one last project."

Jo stared at him. She had spent years begging him for this. All she wanted to do was go to school, get her degree, start a business, and pay taxes like a normal person! Not playing White Rabbit for her father's secret gambling ring and breaking people's fingers when they didn't pay. Not pickpocketing to make a little money on the side, or breaking into empty houses on the weekends. She didn't want to be a criminal—she wanted to be normal. This might be her chance.

On the other hand, it might be the job she got caught on, the one that put her in prison for the rest of her life.

But it might also free her. For real. It wasn't like she hadn't ever done jobs for her father before, and this time, he was offering to pay her what she really wanted—an education. He sure knew how to manipulate her.

"What's the catch?" she asked.

"No catch," Nash said. "Other than that the job might take a few days. I'm not entirely sure. But it's up to you. I'm not going to make you. If you won't do it, I'll find someone else."

Jo frowned. A few days? She might miss class. But she could make up class, especially if her dad was going to pay for a full degree.

"Okay," she agreed. "One last job, and then I'm done."

"Good girl," Nash said. "Now come with me to Mason's house and I'll tell you the details."

CHAPTER 5

Quin growled under his breath as he removed his shoes and dumped water out of them. This was the fourth time today that he had landed in a swamp stinking of sulfur and overrun with swamp rats, and it was not doing anything for his mood. How many different species of swamp rat did the Oliphants need to breed? There were white ones in the first swamp, purple ones in the second swamp, ones the size of a mid-sized human in the third—and in the most recent one—fire! They could breathe fire! It was enough to drive a man batty—or ratty.

"You're back!" John's voice echoed through the room, startling Quin out of his annoyed reverie.

"What are you doing here?" Quin asked, his voice as deep and threatening as he could make it. He did not have the energy to deal with John's chipperness today.

"Just came to say hi, old friend!" John said cheerfully. His tie today was half pink and half blue, with a large hippopotamus-like creature in the center of it.

"Well, I say bye," Quin retorted. Wet feet, burned pants, soaked in sweat, and operating on far too little sleep, Quin could think of a dozen places he would rather be right now, and none of them involved John.

"Now, now," John said, his pleasant attitude unrelenting. "No need to get snippy with me, Grouchy MacGroucherson. I only wanted to see how you were doing. You're soaked, I see. More swamps? Maybe you'd like some company on the next one?" He held up a pair of work boots. "Look what I brought!"

"Who'd you borrow those from?" Quin asked. The shoes looked a couple sizes too large for John.

"Oh, they're Pete's," John replied cheerfully. "So which Door is next?"

Quin carefully rolled the Door into its cylinder and typed a few notes into the computer. It spat out a sticker. He slapped it on the tube, which he tossed into the "Completed" bin.

"You're not supposed to go with me," Quin replied. "It's against regulation. You'll probably just cause problems."

"Come on," John wheedled. "I'll be fine. I've gone through Doors hundreds of times!"

"Aren't you supposed to be working on something else?" Quin tried again.

"My team is putting together that device you suggested," John said. "And I'm on break!"

Quin shook his head. He was too tired to argue.

"That one." He pointed to the next in the bin. John pulled it out and began to unreel it, while Quin reset the hover cam that would follow him through.

"I'm ready!" John exclaimed, after taking off his shoes and slipping on Pete's. They were too big, but John was able to tighten the laces so they wouldn't fall off.

Quin stepped through the Door.

He stood on a ledge overlooking a massive mountain range with higher peaks than he had ever seen, each with strange, jagged edges. The sun sat low on the horizon, and dozens of different colors streaked across the expanse of sky—marigold and blood orange, buttercup yellow and violent red—and then it all blurred and blended together where the sunset met the night in deep blues and indigos, spotted only by the glittering white of barely visible stars.

The mountains themselves were shades of periwinkle and forest greens, and rose and fell as far as Quin could see. Tall trees stretched into the air, giving the mountains additional shape and depth, and he could just barely see a waterfall crashing down the side of one of the great hills. A grey mist hovered in the valleys and wind rushed past undeterred.

He moved forward, almost enthralled by the scene before him. A sense of peace and calm settled into his chest, and a feeling of relaxation pervaded even his most worried thoughts.

"It's beautiful," John breathed, standing next to him.

But something wasn't right. Quin frowned, closing his eyes. He slowly breathed the air, and listened. He almost hadn't heard it under the rushing of the wind, but there it was—a low rumble, like thunder, except that there were no visible storms brewing. He looked all around, searching for the source of the sound but could see nothing. Then the ground beneath his feet began to shake and tremble.

They stood on pebbles and dirt—only now the pebbles bounced and shifted as the ground growled and roared.

"Uh oh," John said, taking a step back. The ledge they stood on shifted slightly.

"Get back to the Door!" Quin yelled. He ran backwards, but his feet kept slipping, slipping, as the ledge tilted and angled down, away from the Door. "Go!"

John took a flying leap and landed in a heap right next to the Door.

"Go!" Quin shouted again, and the next thing he knew, he was alone and John had disappeared. Quin stumbled and fell, the ground falling, sliding beneath his feet. He took a deep breath and leaped as the ledge collapsed out from under him. His fingers grasped the empty air where the rock had been, and then the rock itself; he hung, swinging wildly, trying to get himself under control. *Breathe deep, focus on the objective—the Door.*

Slowly, he pulled himself up until his chin was just over the top of the ledge. The Door was within touching distance, if only he could get himself up onto the ledge. He stretched out one arm as far as it could go and stuck his hand through the Door. There, he felt another hand grab it and pull, pull, pull, and ever so slowly Quin struggled up and over the ledge.

He glanced over his shoulder one more time and saw that it wasn't only his mountain that had moved—they had all moved. The shuddering and groaning grew only louder, and Quin knew beyond the shadow of a doubt that this world, no matter how beautiful, was dying.

He lurched forward in a controlled roll and landed on the floor of the Archaeology Room.

"Thanks," he gasped.

"Good thing I was there," John said, a small frown on his face. "We really should have teams doing this, not individuals doing it alone. I'll talk to Mr. Drake."

Quin nodded and took inventory of his body. Both feet, both legs, both hands and arms, and a head. He was fine. But that was the closest he had come to death in a long time. A burst of energy rushed through him and he felt a small smile grow on his face. He had enjoyed it. Slowly, he pulled himself to his feet and typed into the computer: "WARNING: DO NOT ENTER. DEAD PLANET."

It printed out a little sticker as John reeled up the Door.

"I think I might need a break," Quin said, and strode out of the room.

*****

He stared at the unlit cigarette in his hand. He shouldn't smoke it. He hadn't smoked in years. He knew he shouldn't but somehow everything was awful, even though it wasn't. He had a good job, good friends, and was even on speaking terms with his dad. He was learning new things daily, he got to explore new places and see new things, but he wasn't content, and he was annoyed at himself because of it. He should be happy. He should be grateful. He should be fulfilled.

But right now, he kind of hated everything.

He almost wished he had fallen off that cliff.

At least he had the common sense to contemplate smoking in a rather private location. He stood behind the Globe in one of the gardens, surrounded by tall carefully manicured bushes. Someone could probably see him from the top floors of the Globe, but they wouldn't be able to see the poison stick he twirled in his fingers.

"You Quin Black?"

Quin quickly hid the cigarette in the pocket of his jacket and looked up. "Who are you?" he asked.

"My name is Mason," the woman replied. Her dark hair was piled up on her head in elegant braids, and she was broad shouldered and well-muscled. In fact, he thought she might be quite an adversary if they ever had reason to fight. A man, shorter than her but equally as muscular, stood next to her.

"What can I do for you?"

"I need you to come with me, please," she replied.

"I'm working," he answered.

"Don't look like you're working to me," her friend added. "Looks like you're smoking."

"I'm on break and have to go back," Quin replied. "Can this wait?"

"I'm afraid not," Mason replied. "You owe my employer a lot of money."

Quin frowned. "I don't owe anybody money."

"If you won't come," she said, "we'll have to make you."

"I'd like to see you try," Quin said.

"If that's what you want." Mason held a small tube up to her lips and blew. Quin felt a small prick in his neck.

"What did you—" he started to say, but then the world got fuzzy and blurry and bubbly and black.

*****

When Quin woke up he was on the floor. His hands were untied and his head throbbed. A bit of sunlight came shining in the window. He seemed to be propped up on some kind of couch.

"Awake already?" a voice asked.

41

He squinted up to see Mason towering over him. "Most people take another two hours to process that much tranq. You've only been out for about 45 minutes."

"It's my superpower," he muttered, trying to take better notes of his surroundings. It looked like a normal living room—probably in a rough part of town going by the bars on the front door—but it appeared to have a kitchen and a bathroom, and he could see a row of houses through the window, so he hadn't been dragged into the woods somewhere.

"Are you ready to talk?" she asked.

"Fine," Quin replied.

"You owe us money," Mason said.

"What for?" Quin asked.

"Did you or did you not sign up to play a game of White Rabbit last night?"

Quin frowned.

"And did you or did you not walk out in the middle of the game?"

Quin's frown deepened.

"And did you or did you not wager ten thousand dollars that you would win?"

"There was an explosion," Quin said. "You expected people to stay even though there was an explosion?"

"You wagered ten thousand dollars and walked out on the game," Mason said. "It's called gambling for a reason, and it's not designed to be fair."

Quin shifted his weight so he was in more of an upright position and rubbed his eyes. This was insane, ridiculous. But he kind of understood. Their property had been destroyed, they had to rebuild, and the best place to get money was from losers like him.

"I'm not paying," he said. "That's ridiculous."

"You will pay, or we'll make you," she said.

"How are you going to do that?"

She shrugged. "You don't need all of your fingers, do you? Maybe a couple toes."

"We can sell 'em on the black market," her friend suggested, laughing.

Mason shook her head at him. "No," she said, "that's not funny." She turned her attention back to Quin. "So what'll it be—limbs or money?"

"Limbs, I guess," he replied. That would be a lot cheaper to fix—he had health insurance. "But there's nothing stopping me from walking out. You didn't even tie me up."

She showed him her gun. "I'll shoot you in the back."

"I see." Quin knew he could handle her if he wanted to, and probably anyone else that was here too. But he was curious—would she actually follow through with cutting off a limb? "Limbs, then," he said.

Mason slid a knife out of her pocket. A little frown had appeared on her forehead, like she hadn't expected this kind of reaction. She grabbed Quin's hand and placed it on the arm of the couch. He didn't resist. She held the knife over his pinky finger, hovering. He didn't flinch, didn't resist.

"Is there something wrong with you?" she asked.

He shrugged. "Probably. You did catch me thinking about smoking."

"You're not even fazed at the thought of losing a finger."

He shrugged again. "Nope."

"Mason, Mason," a voice said from the stairwell. "What are you doing?"

A man stepped into view—Nasty Nash himself. He had a scar down his face that was neatly stitched up. "You can't go carving up Quin Black for a measly ten grand. Don't be stupid. Someone would notice." He turned his face towards Quin. "I'm Andrew Nash—you might know me as Nasty Nash."

"Ah yes," Quin replied. "Pleasure to officially meet you."

Mason stepped back away from Quin and slipped the knife into her pocket. She seemed agitated, probably because her boss had interrupted her rather pathetic attempt to extort money from Quin.

"So I understand you owe me money," Nash began, "but I also understand that it was due to some very unfortunate circumstances."

"I don't think I owe you money—"

"Ah but you do," Nash interrupted. "The rules of the game state that if you leave the table for any reason, you are responsible for payment in full. But I understand that the circumstances were, in fact, unfortunate, and you had a difficult decision to make—stay at the table and get caught by police, or leave. So I'm willing to offer you a deal."

Quin thought for a moment. A deal with Nash was probably a bad idea, but depending on what it was, it would probably get him out of this while also making his life a tad bit more interesting. Anything would be better than the boredom he was suffering right now. "What are you offering?"

"I have a small problem," Nash said. "Well, I have several problems, but most of them are not your concern. This problem involves some items I recently acquired from a lovely old woman who owed me money and had refused to pay multiple times. She finally offered these items as an alternative form of payment, and being that I am a generous and compassionate man, I agreed. However, I am in need of some assistance in exploring them."

"Exploring?"

Nash gestured to Mason who gave him an irritated expression. "Go get them, please."

"We can't trust him," she argued.

"I know," Nash replied. "Go get them."

Mason disappeared into the kitchen and returned with three very battered looking cylinders. They were brownish grey—the same type Quin had been working with at the Globe. Whether they actually had Doors stored in them or not remained to be seen.

"I see," Quin said. "You want me to find out what is on the other side of those Doors."

"Yes."

"Why not send one of your henchmen—Mason, here, for example?"

"She might find something so wonderful that she wouldn't come back," Nash said.

"Or she might die." Quin added, thinking it through a little more. "And you might miss her but you wouldn't miss me."

"Too true. But the truth is, I can't trust anyone like I can trust you."

"What makes you think you can trust me? Even if I go and come back, I could lie to you about what's on the other side."

"You have a job and a career," Nash said. He pulled a piece of paper out of his pocket. "You also gamble illegally and owe me ten thousand dollars. If you go through the Doors and die—well, I don't care. If you go through and then come back and lie to me about it, then you will lose that career and all of your friends." He handed the paper to Quin. It was a photograph of Quin playing White Rabbit. Nash handed him a second photo. It was of him from several years ago, also playing White Rabbit. Together, the photos were very incriminating, implying that his choice to play White Rabbit last night was not just a one-time bad choice, but a regular habit. He was good, Quin had to give him that.

"I see," Quin said.

"I shouldn't think that it would be much of a decision," Nash said. "From what I hear, you're quite good at popping through Doors, making an assessment, and coming back. What's the hold-up?"

Quin shrugged. "I guess there isn't any." He did this every day. Three Doors were nothing. And it would be a lot cheaper than paying the ten grand Nash was asking, or getting into a fight that left multiple people injured. Or having limbs removed, for that matter. "Only that I have to get back to work. They'll miss me."

Nash looked at Quin. "Will they though?"

Quin thought about it. He was locked away in a tiny room, in the back of the building, sorting uncategorized Doors, and he had been doing this for days. The only person who came to visit him was John, and if he had a busy afternoon, he might not even notice Quin was missing. Plus, this was a much more interesting task than his forays through confiscated Doors—even if he was technically doing the same thing.

"Eh," Quin grunted. "Let's do it."

"Fantastic," Nash replied. "But there is one more thing."

Quin sighed. There always was.

"Just to make sure you actually come back, you'll be taking my daughter with you."

CHAPTER 6

"Hi," Jo said, stepping into the room. Quin's eyebrow twitched, which she assumed indicated his surprise. "I'm Jo."

"Uh, Quin," he replied, reaching out to shake her hand.

She was relieved he pretended not to recognize her. It was better Nash didn't know Quin had rescued her from the explosion. He already had enough leverage for them both.

Jo had changed into boots and a jacket, and carried a backpack filled with food and supplies. Quin was also wearing heavy duty boots, which she noticed were surprisingly wet, and clothes designed to be adaptable to the elements.

"Fantastic!" Nash said. "Then we start right away. Jo's all ready, you're all ready. Let's go!"

Jo stepped forward. Part of her was nervous—she had never done anything like this before, and she still wasn't sure her dad wouldn't end up screwing her over in the end. On the other hand, it was kind of exciting—exploring new places through these Doors. Plus she would finally get to go to college. She was curious to see what strange people or animals or plants might be on the other side, and if she was going to do this with anyone, Quin seemed like the right person. At least he already knew what he was doing.

"I'll go first," Quin said. "Wait two minutes, then follow. That way, if there is anything dangerous on the other side, or if the air isn't breathable, I can come back and warn you before you step through."

Jo nodded. She watched Quin step forward and disappear through the Door.

She counted to a hundred, then stepped forward. It was a

strange feeling, being in the Door—like she was alive and not alive at the same time, floating but also not floating. And it was so dark she couldn't see anything except the little sparks behind her eyelids that were probably just neurons in her brain firing—but it only lasted a fraction of a second and then she was suddenly… somewhere else. Mason's house had disappeared along with Mason and Nash, and she stood, knee deep in water, looking out at a muggy, green swamp.

"Not another one," she heard Quin grumble from in front of her. "What is it with all these stupid swamps? Who on earth would think to themselves, 'You know where I want to go on vacation every year? A swamp!' or, 'You know what would be great? If we bred fire-breathing rats in a swamp!' Insane people, that's who!"

Jo couldn't see any rats from where she stood, but if there were fire-breathing ones, she definitely wanted to. She didn't care a bit that she was knee-deep in mud—look at the sky, a *different* sky! One she had never seen—and a different sun! This one was darker than theirs, redder. And the plants—with spikes and spherical flowers and vibrant blueish green leaves, some of them rectangular. Tall trees with straight, purple and grey trunks reached high out of the water. She would have argued with Quin's grumbling, but Quin mostly appeared to be talking to himself. He had waded a little way out in the swamp, and now turned look at Jo.

"Let's go back," he said. "This is worthless."

"No," she said. "We need to explore. What are we going to do—go tell Nash, 'Oh hey, Dad, we ended up in a swamp so we decided to come back without looking around?' No way."

Quin stared at her, shoulders squared, about as imposing as a person could look when knee-deep in vile-smelling swamp water.

Jo was shaking in her boots, but luckily Quin couldn't see inside her boots, so she put on her stubborn face and crossed her arms. She knew if he wanted to, he could toss her over his shoulder and drag her back home. But to her surprise, all he said was, "Fine, then," and began mucking through the swamp as fast as he could.

Keeping up was hard work, but Jo did her best. As they moved deeper into the swamp, she noted that it didn't smell that bad—it had become sweet and light, like orange and honey. But the water was still deep, filled with roots and rocks. She fell twice, and was soon up to her shoulders in muck. But instead of finding it uncomfortable or stressful, she found it funny. A surprising bit of laughter began to bubble up inside her. She tried to keep it down, but then, as she watched, Quin tripped and his whole body flew forward—as if in slow motion—and he landed with a huge splash.

She couldn't help it. She burst out laughing, and the laughter came from deep within, a hearty, throaty laugh that shook every part of her. She howled until tears poured down her cheeks.

Quin slowly pulled himself up out of the muck, and when Jo had stopped laughing enough to open her eyes, she could see that Quin wore a small, if sheepish, grin on his face.

"Oops," was all he said, and before she knew it, she was laughing as if to burst all over again.

She took a few gasping breaths for air and then gestured in front of them. "We should keep going," she said, still grinning.

"Agreed," Quin replied, a smile still hovering around his lips. He turned and strode forward through the muck and the water, swiping vines out of their way and trying to avoid the deepest areas of muck. After another few minutes of walking, Quin pointed ahead of them. "I think I see something," he said, and quickened his pace.

Jo followed, trying not to start laughing again, and was surprised to see a wooden path ahead of them. It was built into the swamp, as if to allow someone to walk over the surface of the water, and it ran perpendicular to the direction they had been travelling.

Quin dragged himself up onto it and then reached down to help Jo up. They stood, dripping, and looked around.

"I guess we should follow the path, then," Jo said, grinning. She still felt an overwhelming urge to chuckle, but tried to hold it back. She didn't want Quin thinking she was crazy. "But will we be able to get back to the Door? I don't want to get lost."

"I can navigate back," Quin replied. "Which way?"

Jo looked down the path in both directions, then gestured right. Quin strode off so quickly that Jo had to jog to keep up.

Jo passed the time by observing the plants. At first, she thought they looked like normal hot weather plants—and after all, she had only gotten to basic perennials and vegetables in her horticultural studies. But when she looked more carefully, she noticed that there was one viney plant that grew in and around all the other plants. It wove through the water plants, winding its way up the trees. It peeked through the flowers and even sometimes stretched across the wooden trail. The four-leafed vine was mostly green, but when she looked closer, she noticed tiny flakes of red spotted every part of the plant—stems, leaves, and buds.

But as they walked along the path, she saw that the speckles had, at some point, turned blue. She sneezed a few times, and noticed that the air smelled fresh and clean, like a creek was running somewhere nearby surrounded by soft grasses and pine trees. The laughter she had felt began to dissipate, and she suddenly felt a strong longing to go home. She was here, in this strange swamp on a strange planet—there could be dangerous animals or people hiding in the flora and fauna around her and she wouldn't know it! And what if Quin couldn't get them back? What if they were trapped? They should head back to the Door before anything terrible happened. Home was safe. Home was home.

"I think we should go home," she said abruptly, hoping that Quin didn't find her sudden conversation startling.

"I'm getting the same feeling," Quin said. He had a slight frown on his face. "Let's see what's in that clearing ahead, and if there's nothing we'll go home. Sound alright?"

Jo really would have preferred to turn around right then, but it made sense, and they wanted to at least be able to tell Nash that they had tried, right?

When they stepped into the clearing, Jo gasped. It was beautiful. A small, perfectly landscaped hill rose from the swampy wetlands with grass, flowers, and bushes growing all over it. Six houses sat on the hill, each a different color—red, purple, blue, green, yellow, and orange—like a rainbow.

"Stay close," Quin said, walking forward.

Jo nodded and crept up behind Quin, who had slowed down. The nearest house was red. Quin peered through the windows, and Jo copied him. There was furniture inside, but no people.

"I'll try the door." Quin turned the handle and it swung open.

A sign hung from the ceiling in perfect view of the door. "Welcome," it said, "to the house of laughter."

They stepped inside, looking around cautiously. It was wonderfully furnished, Jo thought, with warm colors and soft, comfortable-looking furniture. It had an open floor plan with a kitchen on one side and a huge fireplace on the other. It hadn't occurred to Jo that it might get cold here sometimes. Another door on the back of the house led out to the purple cabin.

She breathed deeply as she entered the house. The aroma drifted softly past, of honey and oranges and bamboo. She felt happiness well up inside, and a smile hovered around her lips. She wanted to laugh, but Quin was already on his way out.

He strode through the house and opened the back door, heading up to the next cabin without hesitation. The sign inside the purple cabin read: "Welcome to the house of longing."

Jo breathed in as she entered. This one smelled of a creek, soft grasses, and pine trees. It had the same floor plan as the others, but with darker colors. A rotten banana lay on the counter. Quin poked at the banana, then continued through the door to the next cabin.

Jo paused for a moment and looked around. She felt torn—she wanted to stay here somehow, but she also wished to go home, to go to school and find a career. She wanted to build herself a safe place that was all hers. But it seemed that right now, all she was destined for was to follow Quin around.

The next cabin was filled with handkerchiefs, strewn all over the building. The walls were painted in blues and greys and black, and the sign read, "Welcome to the house of grief." It smelled of rain, with a strange hint of must and mold that Jo found oddly satisfying. She thought of Stanky and a tear rolled down her cheek.

Quin didn't wait at all in this house, but walked out the back almost as quickly as he had entered. Jo paused before stepping out the door, but Quin grabbed her hand and pulled her forward.

The green cabin's sign read, "Welcome to the house of contentment," and there were boxes of non-perishable food everywhere. Quin paused and grabbed a handful of granola bars.

"Do you think these are safe?" he asked. "I'm starving."

Jo threw herself into one of the chairs, wiping the tear from her eye. It was extremely comfortable, and she felt the dampness of her clothes beginning to melt away. It smelled of cinnamon and laundry detergent. "This is the most comfortable chair I've ever sat in," she said, noticing that Quin had already begun to eat the granola bars, even though she had never answered his question. He strode into the living room and plopped down on the couch opposite her.

"Wow," he said. "You're right."

"So what do you think these houses are?" Jo asked.

"Mood houses," Quin replied.

"Well obviously," Jo said. "Each one is clearly labelled. But I mean, what are they actually for?"

"Changing your mood," Quin said.

Jo scowled at him. How could a house change a mood? That didn't make any sense. Of course, a house that you went to a lot might make you feel more comfortable, or a place where someone had died might make you feel sad. But these houses were just kind of colorfully generic.

"What do you mean?" she asked.

"Well," Quin replied, "I figured out where we are."

"That would have been helpful for you to mention."

"We are on a planet called Nalada. This is a ring of mood houses. Those plants that grow out in that swamp—skap, they're called—have an actual, physiological effect on the mood of people from Sagitta. It doesn't affect all species the same way, but..."

"Wait," Jo said, frowning. "Those plants out there can make me feel happy or sad or grumpy? By—what? Touching them?"

"Not even," Quin replied. "Breathing their pollen. These houses probably have diffusers in them somewhere so that when you're in them, you're feeling a particular way."

"Oh." Jo was surprised. She hadn't ever heard of anything like this before. But that explained the changing smells too. The laundry detergent smell—must be what contentment smelled like. She had only been semi-interested in horticulture before—the career path was just the most opposite thing she could think of from her father's lifestyle—but now she found herself wanting to learn more.

"A few centuries ago," Quin said, "this was actually a pretty big problem. People were selling skap like drugs, and people would always be happy and never feel anything else—pain, sorrow, suffering. It's great, until you realize that pain and suffering opens the door for progress. Anyway, all the Doors here were closed, and we had a bit about it in our training, because there are still some illegal Doors that come here. People use them to sell moods."

"So when I was laughing so hard in the swamp—was that the skap making me do that?"

"Yup."

"And that feeling of wanting to go home?"

"Yup. And certain mixes of different moods can make you feel a range of other moods—like a color palette," Quin added.

"Wow, Dad is going to be happy about this," Jo said. He would be ecstatic, over the moon. He could make millions off of this—assuming he could do it without getting caught. She felt a little bad. This stuff could kill society—and she could get in trouble for it, even if Nash was the one selling it.

"Nope," Quin said. "We can't tell him. We can't have this stuff back on the market."

"What do we tell him then?"

"That it's a swamp. Useless. Wet. Empty. Poisonous bugs."

She frowned. Nash wasn't going to be happy if he thought all he'd gotten was access to a swamp. But she agreed with Quin. This stuff really shouldn't be sold on the black market—which she knew was the first thing her father would do with it. It wouldn't be good for her, Nash, or society. Plus, they still had two Doors to go through—one of them would surely have something else of value.

"Okay," she said.

It was Quin's turn to frown. "That's it?" he asked. "You're going along with this?"

"What else am I supposed to do?" she asked. "This is dangerous stuff. I believe you. I don't want it in Pomegranate City any more than you."

"But, aren't you part of his gambling thing?" Quin pressed.

"Sort of." She frowned. "But I don't want to be." She wasn't sure how much she wanted to tell this stranger who had saved her and was now exploring the universe with her in a very strange twist of events, but she felt safe and comfortable with him—or was it the house making her feel that way? Her mouth opened without her permission. "I want to go to school. For horticulture."

"Really?" Quin acted surprised. "But you were the White Rabbit—I thought you were so involved in the operation that you were in trouble or something."

"Nah." Jo knew what Quin was referring to. The White Rabbit was usually played by a slave or someone who owed the dealer money, because at the end of the game the winner had to kill the White Rabbit in order to fully win. "I wear body armor."

Quin barked out a short laugh. "Wow. Smart. Also, stupid."

She shrugged. "He gives me a thirty percent cut if I do it, so he doesn't have to find someone else. Plus, hardly anyone wins. And if they get to the point of throwing the knife, I duck. They're usually too drunk to notice. I have a couple scars though, on my arms."

"Why horticulture?" Quin asked.

"Why not? It's legal," Jo said, checking the items off on her fingers. "I can start my own business. It's not too hard. It's at least a little interesting. And I only need a few plants to hit restart every time my father tries to burn my business down."

"Sounds like a rough life," Quin said.

"And I suppose yours is easier?"

Quin looked out the window. "Seems like it should be, but it doesn't feel that way."

"Is that why you're gambling?"

"I'm bored. With everything. I miss adrenaline rushes. I miss taking risks—not knowing if I'm going to survive or not."

"Aren't you in the military, though? Aren't you on some kind of Door task force? Isn't that a little risky?"

"I suppose," Quin said. "I guess I did almost die this morning. A planet started crumbling under my feet. And you know what's weird? I liked it. I wished I had gotten caught up in the earthquake—but I didn't. I got back safe." He sighed and leaned his head back against the couch. "I don't know what I want. I have this general sense of not doing enough, not being strong enough, not caring enough, not… I don't know, something. Like I'm empty."

Jo nodded. "I get that."

They sat in silence for a while, both looking out the window. Jo wasn't sure why she had told Quin about her life and her goals, and she wasn't sure why Quin had admitted his dissatisfaction with life to her, but she had a feeling it had something to do with the Contentment House. She felt like she could stay here all day, with Quin or without him. But her mind was largely empty, soft, safe. It was peaceful to sit and say nothing, to not mind the bad things and not be passionate about the good. She felt calm and at ease. This might not reflect the truest version of herself, but this feeling—she wouldn't forget it.

Finally she asked, "So what are the other colors for?"

"Orange is rage," Quin replied quietly, "so let's skip that one. Yellow is cheerfulness, I think, or hope. Something like that."

"So there's not one for love or hate?"

"No." Quin shook his head. "My understanding is that those are compilations of emotions—we really only feel a few things purely, like happiness, sadness, hope, longing, and anger—I think. And all other emotions are combinations. Like love might be cheerfulness and hope with laughter and contentment, maybe a little sadness mixed in, and a lot of longing. See what I mean?"

"Yeah!" This was an interesting game. "And hate would be rage and sadness with longing—or something like that."

"I think it would probably be better if we went back," Quin said. "There aren't many civilizations on this planet, but I think it would be better if we avoided running into them."

Jo nodded. Who knew what kind of people they would be?

"Besides," he added, "we still have two more Doors."

They stood together, heading out the front door onto the porch. The swamp really was beautiful, Jo thought, looking out from the porch over the green landscape, with the colorful flowers, the rectangular leaves, the vibrancy and life. The bugs buzzed about and the birds twittered, and Jo smiled a little to herself and watched.

"Look at this," Quin said. He had wandered down to the other end of the porch and was looking at something that hung on the wall. It was a map. "It shows that path we were on" —he pointed— "and if we go a little further, it runs past the Door, out of sight from where we were."

"What's that down there?" she asked, pointing to a larger blob.

"I think that's a city," Quin replied. "The path runs right to it."

"I guess we'd better head back then," Jo said, "before anyone decides to wander down to their cabins."

"Agreed," Quin replied, leading her away from the house and back towards the path.

Jo glanced back at the green house over her shoulder, wishing she could go inside to sit and relax again. That feeling of peace, calm, serenity—that would be a feeling she would pursue for the rest of her life.

CHAPTER 7

Quin found himself quite irritable when they arrived back at the Door. He was soaking wet, covered in bug bites, and very annoyed at himself for telling Jo as much as he had. All he had wanted was to sit down for a few minutes and eat, but apparently the "Contentment" house also included spilling your guts to whomever happened to be sitting across from you.

At least she had shared too, so he wasn't alone in his annoyance.

He had been quite impressed with Jo so far. She had kept up with him the entire time, hadn't complained once, asked good questions about where they were and what they were doing, and didn't chatter on all the time like some people—ahem, John. He thought she might actually make a good partner to go Door surfing with—which was good, since they still had two Doors left to explore.

They crawled back into Mason's living room, reeking of swamp gases. Quin felt an unnecessary amount of pleasure at the way the bugs flew off of their clothes and buzzed around the room, and the putrid water dripped from their pants and boots and soaked into the carpet. He moved farther into the room to spread the mess around as much as possible.

"It was a swamp," Jo said immediately, shaking her head. "Worthless." She sounded confident and assured—a convincing liar. Water flew in all directions as her long hair swung around her head. Quin was suddenly extremely grateful that he didn't have any hair—one less problem for him to worry about.

Mason had a look of horror on her face as she stared at his boots, which squelched every time he moved his feet.

"Mind if I change before we go through the next one?" Jo ran off without waiting for Quin's response.

Mason threw a towel at Quin, who rubbed his head and his face, and then dumped the water out of his boots all over the floor. Nash watched, clearly not worried about the mess, while Mason wrung her hands behind him.

"A swamp?" Nash asked, leaning forward. "Anything good there? Valuable?"

"We hiked for over an hour," Quin lied. "Didn't find anything."

"You were gone for two hours." Nash frowned.

"Yes," Quin replied, letting his feeling of annoyance flow into his voice. "That's how hiking for an hour works. You hike away from the Door for an hour, and then you hike back. We even made a loop in case we missed something."

Nash scowled. "Well that's not worth the money she owed."

Quin was relieved Nash believed them. Now, he had to find a way to get it safely stowed away at the Globe.

"My guess," Quin said, "is that there used to be something there and now there's not. Your best bet is to dump this out with next year's hazardous waste, or let the Globe have it so they can stick it in their stacks of useless Doors."

"Jo!" Nash called. "You done yet?"

She came thundering down the stairs in dry clothes. She still smelled like swamp gases, and her hair was full of sticks, but she looked much happier and more comfortable.

"Hey, those are mine," Mason complained.

"I know," Jo said cheerily. "And they look a lot better on me. Ready to go through the next Door, Quin?"

"Wait a second," Nash said. "Quin here says wasn't anything of value in the swamp. That what you think?"

Jo nodded. "I'd say the woman fleeced you, Dad—unless your idea of a vacation is a swamp full of rotting tree roots and poisonous frogs. They also have bugs, if you're into that sort of thing." She shrugged. "There probably used to be something there, way back a long time ago, but it's disappeared since. And you couldn't convince me to go back—not in a million years."

Nash sighed and sat back on the couch. "Fine," he said.

Quin unrolled the next Door and looked back at Jo. She gave him a thumbs-up and he stepped through the Door.

*****

Everything was white. Sparkling, shining, brilliant, blindingly white. Quin stepped back for a moment, shielding his eyes, almost bumping into Jo as she came through the Door behind him.

"Ouch!" Jo exclaimed, covering her eyes. "Why is it so bright?"

"Please step forward," a robotic voice intoned, "and check in at the front desk."

As they moved away from the Door, the light faded a little, and Quin began to see the room around them. Wide windows filled the walls and arched ceilings, letting in the blinding light from outside. Everything was spotless, except where Quin's feet left muddy footprints. A few plants stood along the walls, their dark green a stark contrast to the whiteness of everything else. In the center of the room, a desk—also white—appeared to be manned by a robot of some kind.

"What is that?" Jo asked, leaning forward and squinting towards the figure.

"Please step forward," the voice said again.

Quin stepped up to the front desk, and the humanoid robot turned to look at him. Its face would have been smooth and white, but someone had drawn on eyes and a mouth with what looked like a red child's crayon. "Welcome to Dr. Oliphant's laboratory. Please step forward to get sanitized."

There were hundreds of Dr. Oliphants, Quin knew, but only one Dr. Oliphant was famed for his robots. He had disappeared several hundred years ago, and there had been much speculation about where he had gone. If this was the Dr. Oliphant Quin thought, then the sanitization process was safe and used by nearly every hospital and research facility he had been in.

Jo looked at Quin with a mildly panicked look in her eyes.

"It's fine," Quin said. "I think they are talking about Dr. Lake Oliphant, inventor. If so, then I've been through his sterilization process before and it's fine."

"Where are we, though?" Jo asked.

"I think we are in an interdimensional space," Quin replied, "but we'll have to take a look around before I'll know for sure."

Two doors slid up to the right of the desk to reveal sanitization rooms.

"Please remove your dirty garments and put on the robes provided for you," the robot said.

Quin stepped into the first booth and the door slid closed behind him. He didn't wait to see what Jo did. Inside, he removed his clothing and placed it in a bin with a picture of dirty clothes on it. A warm mist began to spray out of nozzles at the top of the room, and the mud and dirt rushed down his body and through a drain. It felt wonderful. He hadn't realized how badly he wanted a shower. The mist stopped and a fan began to blow, quickly drying him off. Then a drawer slid out of the wall with a white pair of pants, underwear, and a shirt folded neatly in it. Quin slipped them on. As soon as he finished, a door on the opposite wall slid up and Quin stepped out.

This room was also white, though not so blinding as the previous. It looked as though there were fewer windows and more plants. Quin glanced down at his arm. If he didn't know that it was a trick of the light, he would have thought that his dark skin had become even darker.

Jo stepped through the sliding door, also wearing white pants and a shirt. "That felt amazing." She still had some sticks in her hair, but otherwise looked much more relaxed.

A different robot stood in front of them. This one also had a face drawn on it with crayon, but one of the eyes was crooked and it only had one eyebrow. Its neck was a simple conduit, likely filled with wires, and its body a long, round egg. It rolled smoothly on four wheels. "Welcome, Dr. Oliphant and friends," the robot said. Quin frowned. Lake Oliphant wasn't here, was he? Quin looked around quickly, to be sure.

"Where are we?" Jo whispered. "And does he think one of us is Dr. Oliphant?"

"I don't know, but this is one of the weirder places I've been, that's for sure." Quin turned his attention to the robot. "Excuse me," he said politely, unsure of how to address it.

"How may I help Dr. Oliphant's friend?" the robot intoned.

"Could you tell us where we are?"

"You have reached Dr. Oliphant's lab."

"If I could ask," Quin pressed. "Which Dr. Oliphant?"

"You have reached the lab of Dr. Lake Oliphant the sixteenth, engineer."

"And what are you?"

"I am a Model 337 Service Bot. I run on an X16 Turbo 554 Engine. My chief function is to serve Dr. Oliphant and his friends while ensuring that the laboratory is maintained at maximum efficiency."

"And what does that other robot do?" Quin asked.

"We are all one," the robot replied.

"What do you mean?"

"We are all one," the robot repeated.

"Well that's creepy," Quin muttered under his breath.

"What does he mean?" Jo asked.

"I think he means that all of the bots here operate with the same cloud server. Like, they all have the same mind, same programming, but different bodies—like a colony of zap ants or something." He turned back to the robot. "What is this lab for?" he asked.

"Please follow me," the robot said. "I will show you." It turned and zoomed down a long hallway, its wheels so well-maintained that it didn't leave any marks on the floor.

"Suppose you wanted to explore the universe, but didn't have the strength or courage to travel," the robot began. "Dr. Oliphant grew ill at a young age, and knew he would never see as much of the universe as he wanted. So he built this place for himself and future scholars to study and learn about different places and cultures without having to go anywhere.

"This is not only a place for research and study, however. Dr. Oliphant uses this laboratory for meditation and relaxation. While the building houses numerous workshops and laboratories, what you will see today encompasses centuries of work on the part of Dr. Oliphant. The Room of Windows is a beautiful homage to the complexity and wonder of the universe, and Dr. Oliphant is proud to share it with two of his closest friends."

This was definitely weird. Why the robots thought Quin and Jo were two of Dr. Oliphant's closest friends, he had no idea, and he was hesitant to follow the robot too much farther into the building. What if it was a trap? What if they were going to get eaten or experimented on?

Then the robot stopped and gestured to a door. "Welcome to the Room of Windows. Please make yourself at home."

The door slid open. They stepped out onto a platform that hovered on the edge of a massive sphere. Without warning, it rushed out into the center so quickly that Quin had to grab onto railing for balance. Every inch of the sphere around them was covered with images—some of forests or jungles, others of cities or villages, deserts, rivers, kitchens, oceans, mountains—and every single one moved, but not like a movie, more like something that was being filmed continuously from the same angle.

Quin looked down at the platform; it appeared to have no controls. "Up," he said, and it rose slowly.

Jo's mouth was agape as she viewed the scene around them. "What is it?" she asked.

Quin didn't answer. He scanned the images, one after another, looking for something, anything that might tell him exactly what he was seeing. And then, there it was.

"Left, down, left," he said, and the platform moved diagonally down until they stared at the six cabins sitting on a grassy hill, each painted a different color.

"Is that...?" Jo asked, pointing at the image.

"I think so," Quin replied. It was a window into Nalada and the mood swamp.

"So, if I had been standing here while you were exploring the houses," Jo asked, "would I have been able to see you?"

Quin shook his head. "I don't know. Maybe? Let's look for other places that seem familiar." He looked to the left and right, and then said clearly, "Move left, slowly." The hover platform began to drift and Quin carefully studied each window they passed by. One looked out onto a beach and another showed a quiet alleyway in an unknown city. There was a cat napping in a windowsill, a busy highway with hundreds of spherical vehicles speeding along, and a band of dog-eared humanoids playing green and purple instruments. They saw a boat tossed in a heavy storm; a cow lazily munching on chartreuse grass; a classroom filled with a dozen students; a massive mining operation on the side of a mountain; a double-sun sunset over a purple moor.

"Stop," Quin said abruptly as a familiar scene came into view. They stared directly into the Globe. He saw Bob, the alien who managed the front desk, with his six blue arms answering all the phones at once, and there was Mr. Drake, recently appointed Head of Technology at the Globe. And then he saw John, who rushed up to Bob at the front desk, flinging his arms around his head as if the whole world was ending.

And beside it, another window, this time into the Door Room. He could see hundreds of people scurrying about, the Doors themselves barely noticeable in the chaos. It was from an angle Quin had never thought of, slightly above the mess, looking out across the room. It made the room look larger than life—and chaotically beautiful.

"Is that... the Globe?" Jo asked. "I've never been inside, but..."

"It is," Quin replied, frowning slightly. It seemed like a bad idea to have a window into what was supposed to be the most secure room in the Globe. "Left." And the platform moved left again, moving slowly around the sphere, showing them each and every window.

And then Jo said, "Stop," and Quin grimaced. There in front of them was a view of Pomegranate City—a neighborhood—just outside of Mason's house.

"Who's that?" Jo asked. She leaned forward to peer through the window. "Do these windows have sound?"

"Some of the windows may have audio," the robot voice intoned out of nowhere. Jo jumped, startled. "If you see a small blinking red light in the corner, say, 'Sound' and you will be able to hear. Dr. Oliphant found it less than useful to be able to hear through all of them—especially when many of them were so windy."

"Sound," Jo said.

"What do you think you're doing?" a voice asked. It was tinny, as though the voice was coming from very far away—which, Quin supposed, it was.

"That's Mason!" Jo exclaimed.

"I did what you asked!" the other figure retorted. "You can't blame me for that!"

"Uncle Dan?" Jo asked, her mouth agape.

"It's your fault it didn't work," Mason said, this time a little louder. She must have been yelling. "The second fuse didn't catch!"

"You put it together—"

"From your instructions!" Mason threw her hands up into the air. "I have to go. Nash might get suspicious." She leaned forward and kissed Jo's uncle on the lips, and then turned and ran into the house.

"She tried to kill my dad?" Jo threw her hands up, almost hitting Quin in the nose. "*And* she's cheating on him?"

"I guess that was the wrong window to look through," Quin said, raising his eyes.

64

Jo covered her face with her hands, clearly furious.

"Officer Reynolds said that some of the parts used to make the device that blew up my dad's house came from my uncle's shop," she said. "I just can't believe that they would... would... do something like this!"

"You're going to have to calm down before we go back," Quin said. "You can't run out and accuse Mason of attempted murder or she'll just disappear. We'll have to come up with some sort of plan."

Jo took a deep breath. "I know," she said. "I know." Quin watched as her facial muscles clenched and unclenched, and her expression shifted from anger to sadness to frustration and back to anger.

"Tell you what," Quin said, feeling a little sorry for her. She was in a tough spot, with a criminal for a father encouraging her to pursue a life she didn't want. Now she had to decide whether to rat out her father's girlfriend or keep out of the mess entirely. "We have one more Door after this."

Jo nodded.

"After we get back from there, I will find Officer Reynolds and tell her that I came to check on you—since I'm already your alibi for that night—and tell her that I witnessed Mason and your uncle having an argument. I can lead her to investigate them more thoroughly so that you don't have to get involved."

"You would do that?"

Quin shrugged. "Shouldn't be too hard. I did see it, after all." He gestured to the window.

Jo's face lit up.

"You have to promise you won't go crazy on Mason when we get back," Quin said, "or she'll run off. You have to pretend you don't know anything."

"But Dad should know—"

"No," Quin held up his hand to cut her off. "She's been cheating for quite a while, most likely. It's not going to make a difference if your dad doesn't know for another three hours."

"Okay," Jo said. "But you promise to help?"

"Yes," Quin replied.

Jo fell silent as the platform continued to move slowly round and round the sphere. They saw herds of purple deer with twisted horns galloping across the plains. They saw frozen tundra filled with birds, and people wrapped up in heavy skins and furs. They saw fish, swimming and bubbling under the ocean—giant fish and small fish, fish with arms, and fish with no eyes, and fish with a giant bulbous rock for a tail. They saw farmers guiding their cows to the pasture, and vehicles rushing by on a road covered with oil and exhaust; people in long coats and elegant dresses, and a spiked lizard playing with a ball; teenagers and elderly people, nurses and scientists; and through it all Quin's head swam in dizzy swirls—he felt as though he were looking into the heart of the universe.

The platform finally reached the bottom of the sphere, humming, and emerged into a room underneath. This was a smaller room with a few windows that looked out on what Quin imagined to be Dr. Oliphant's favorite places. It was furnished with comfortable couches and chairs, and a bed on one wall.

Quin and Jo stepped off the platform and stood, looking around them.

"What was that?" Jo asked.

"The universe, I think," Quin replied.

He stepped forward and collapsed onto a couch, and Jo settled in next to him. They were silent, staring at the few windows that were down here. One looked out over a waterfall, the water rushing and gushing soundlessly over a rock ledge. Another showed a forest planted with trees growing in straight lines. A light mist hovered over the ground, and a breeze blew it into curls and tendrils. The third window was simply a beach. The water lapped up the sand, and then sank away again, and the sun set in brilliant oranges and purples.

"I could look at these all day," Jo whispered.

"For a lifetime," Quin added. He looked around the room to see if any of the eerie robots had followed them in. Not seeing any, he asked, "What is this place?" in a loud voice, hoping one them would answer.

"This is Dr. Oliphant's private office," a disembodied voice replied. "Here, Dr. Oliphant spends most of his waking and sleeping hours, working on projects of high importance."

"It keeps talking like Dr. Oliphant is still alive," Jo said quietly.

"It's very odd," Quin answered. He glanced over at the bed—it looked for a moment like someone was sleeping there. He stood and strode over; Jo followed. When he pulled back the covers, all he saw were bones. A terrible smell rose from the sheets, and Quin quickly settled them back over the skeleton.

"What was that?" Jo asked, scrunching up her nose and looking away.

"I think we've discovered the remains of Dr. Lake Oliphant," Quin replied solemnly.

"Wow," Jo said, a curious expression on her face. "Creepy."

They walked the perimeter of the room. Tall bookcases filled with textbooks, journals, and rolled up scrolls lined one wall. A large desk covered with papers and notebooks sat in the back corner. A cup of tea sat on it, steaming, as if the robots had just refilled it. Quin reached out and picked up sheet of paper that had fallen to the floor. It was a diagram of some kind of computer storage device, with the words, "Consciousness Generator" on the top.

"All his notes are here," Quin said. "Stuff he invented but didn't have time to build."

"This Door is worth a fortune, then," Jo said in a hushed voice.

"Yes," Quin said, "in more ways than one."

"What do we tell my dad?" she asked.

Quin shrugged. They didn't have a lot of choices. "The truth, I suppose. This Door might make him a rich man, but it won't hurt anyone in the process. And we can't lie for every Door, can we?"

"I guess not." Jo shook her head, eyes still wide. "It's just that, well, those windows look into a lot of places that no one has the right to look into."

Quin shrugged. "But if no one knows—"

Jo cut him off. "It doesn't matter if people know! You might not know that the kid across the street is peeking in your windows when you shower, but it's still an invasion of privacy. And even if these places the windows show are technically public, if the people there don't that they are being watched, it's creepy—it's wrong!"

Quin nodded. She was right. He was used to the Globe and the military invading people's privacy, so it didn't really faze him. He knew he was constantly being monitored and watched, which was why he was so careful to leave things that could track him—like his phone—at home when he went gambling. But she was right. This was a different thing. It wasn't one government agent spying on another, or police trying to catch a criminal. This was a way for any one person to watch another person without their knowledge. It wasn't right.

"I guess we'll have to find a way to steal it back, then," Quin said.

Jo nodded. "I think I can help with that."

They stepped back on the hover platform, and it rose quickly to the exit. They strode down the hallway and went back through the disinfectant chamber. It didn't wash him this time, but instead, simply returned his clothes, clean and dry. That was a pleasant surprise, he thought.

"Goodbye, friends of Dr. Oliphant," the robots said as he and Jo strode towards the Door. "We hope you come again soon!"

"Goodbye, friendly robots," Jo said, waving.

Quin grinned as the sparkling white vanished around him.

CHAPTER 8

Jo felt a rush of anger as she stepped into Mason's living room. Mason had tried to kill Nash! And was cheating on him to boot! But she couldn't show the anger. Quin had promised to help—she had to trust him. She couldn't risk Mason running off. So she shifted her face into calm and tried to focus on how much she loved exploring the other sides of the Doors. There was so much to see in the universe, so much to experience. She suddenly found herself a little jealous of Quin's choice of careers, and thought maybe she should switch away from horticulture and find a way to work at the Globe. But she put that thought out of her head too; it wasn't important right now. What was important was finishing up this task so Quin could go find Officer Reynolds.

"That didn't take long," Nash said, frowning at them. "You were only gone for about forty-five minutes. Decided not to explore, eh?"

"What happened to your clothes?" Mason asked, coming into the room from the kitchen. "They're clean!"

"We explored," Jo said to her dad, ignoring Mason. "It was awesome, smaller than the swamp."

"What was it?" The expression on Nash's face shifted from suspicious to curious and excited.

"It was a lab," Jo replied, looking at Quin who nodded in agreement. "The last remnant of Lake Oliphant's legacy. It had a lot of robots and these beautiful windows that looked out to different places all over the universe."

"Is it safe?" Nash asked.

"Absolutely," Quin replied. "Be careful with it, though. It could be dangerous in the wrong person's hands."

"Also," Jo added, "looks like Lake Oliphant's corpse is in there, and all his notes and inventions."

Nash grinned, pleasure spreading across his face. Jo was reminded, once again, that she didn't like her father very much. He would no doubt sell everything in there as soon as he could find buyers.

"I'm very glad to hear it," he said. "Looks like the old lady came through, after all. And by the way, Jo, the police officer called looking for you. You should get back to her when you're done here."

"Fine," Jo said. That was good. Quin could talk to her sooner rather than later.

"And now the third Door," Quin said, pulling the other canister out and setting it up. He paused and looked at Nash. "And after this my debt is forgiven?"

"Yes, yes," Nash said hurriedly. "Now get going."

Jo could tell that as of this moment, Nash didn't care at all about Quin's debt. He only wanted whatever was on the other side of those Doors.

Quin disappeared with Jo right on his heels.

The room that spread out before them was crowded with hundreds of people. Jo's jaw dropped. It was noisy and colorful, and aliens of all different types bustled about. There were also dozens of what looked like scientists, all wearing lab coats in and among the other people, and as far as she could see, the room was filled with row after row of Doors.

"Pepper eaters," she heard Quin mutter next to her.

A gentleman in a lab coat and colorful tie bounced up to them.

"Oh, hey, Quin!" he said. "What are you doing here?" He looked back and forth from the Door to Quin and his face lit into a huge smile. "Did you find it?" he asked. "Did you find the place this Door lets out?"

70

Quin stared at the man, like a skee crab in a spotlight. "This is the Door you're working on?" he asked.

Then the man's eyes lit on Jo and he frowned slightly. "What is she doing here...?" His frown deepened. "Quin?" Then he grabbed Quin by the arm and dragged him away, through the crowded room. Jo hurried to keep up, trying to avoid the jostle of people that surrounded her on all sides. She had no idea what was going on, and was worried that Quin was in some kind of trouble, and that by association she was in some kind of trouble. But they had to stick together.

The man pulled Quin into a room on the opposite wall, and shut the door behind Jo. It appeared to be a conference room. A large table sat in the center surrounded by chairs, and a coffee bar took up a corner on the far wall.

"What do you think you're doing?" he demanded. "With Nash's daughter?"

Jo's eyes widened. How did he know who she was? Had he been there last night? At Pete's Clocks? She thought back. Quin had been there, Pete, Pete's wife, and another person... yeah, it could have been him.

"John," Quin said, "hold on a minute. Let me think for a second."

"Think? Think!" John was extremely upset, and Jo got the feeling that he was naturally a cheerful person—that this kind of mood was unusual for him. "You tell me, right this minute—*how did you walk through that Door?*"

"I stepped through and was here," Quin muttered.

"WHERE DID YOU GET THE DOOR?" John demanded, almost shouting.

Quin glanced at Jo, and John rounded on her abruptly.

"Tell me right now," John said, putting his face so close to hers that she could feel his breath. "What. Is. Going. On."

Jo shrugged. She didn't have anything to lose, as far as she knew. "My dad asked Quin to help find out where some Doors went, and we ended up here."

John spun around again to look at Quin. "You weren't in the Archaeology Room?"

Quin shook his head.

"We were at my dad's girlfriend's house," Jo offered.

John put his face in his hands. "Ugh, this is a mess."

"Why?" Quin asked.

"Because," John said. "Remember how you suggested we try to fit a very small tracking device through the Door?"

"Yes," Quin replied.

"Well, it worked," John said, "though now that I think about it, that's probably only because you opened it. Anyway, a team of scientists are working with the police to set up a raid and secure the Door. Right now. This very second."

Quin looked at Jo. "Good thing we're here and not there."

"It is *not* good!" John exclaimed. "An entire team of scientists just saw you step out of that Door!" He pointed at Jo. "With her!"

Jo looked back and forth from Quin to John. This seemed serious. She had a feeling that the consequences could end up being more than Quin just losing his job. She thought for a minute—what would be best here? Meek? Bold? Confident? Scared? She decided to go for confident and bold, and adjusted her facial features accordingly.

"Excuse me, sir," she said, reaching out her hand. "I'm Jo Nash."

"John," he replied, a surprised look on his face.

"I'm really sorry to have messed this up," she said, "but honestly, I think the easiest thing to do would be to have us go back through the Door and get caught on the other side."

"Can't have that," John replied. "I'm obligated to report you! If I don't, *I* could get fired."

The door burst open. "John!" a woman in a lab coat called. "It's starting!" Without a moment's hesitation, she turned and left again.

"I can't believe you did this to me," John said, turning to stare into Quin's eyes. His face was red, and Jo could see his hands clenched into fists, the veins in his forehead pulsing. "I thought you were my best friend, but maybe you're too stupid to be my friend!"

Quin shrugged, looking at the floor. Jo was surprised to see that John's words were bothering Quin. She had thought he was basically a duck—everything slid off his impenetrable calm.

John shook his head in disgust. "I guess you'll have to come with me," he said harshly, "and don't do anything I don't tell you to!" He turned and headed back out into the Door Room.

Jo was as overwhelmed stepping out into the chaos as she had been the first time. There were so many Doors! And so many people, and aliens—a thin blue scientist, who was taller than most of the Doors, waved his arms around on other end of the room. A woman in voluminous skirts was dragging a wagon full of children through the crowd. Two men with matching faces appeared to be arguing, with a circle of men surrounding them, who, upon closer inspection, also had the same face as the first two.

It was mindboggling. And she loved it.

Before they made it halfway across the room, a young woman who looked rather frazzled latched onto Quin's arm.

"I'm sorry to bother you, sir," she said, "but there's an old lady here to see you? She says you're her friend and refuses to leave until she talks to you."

"It's no problem, Terry. Who is it?" Quin asked.

"It's—" she began, but was interrupted by a "YOOHOO!" from across the room. A tiny, wrinkly old woman was waving frantically and trying to scurry through the crowd.

"That's her," Terry said, sighing. "I told her to wait, but…"

"It's fine," Quin said. "I'll take care of it."

"What is Mavis Oliphant doing here? How did she even get in here?" John hissed as she wiggled her way through a group of workers having a lunch break. "I don't have time for this!'

Quin didn't have time to answer, as Mavis suddenly stood right in front of them. "Hello, Quin dear—oh hello, Jo. Quin, dear, I needed to have a quick chat with you about something, probably not with Jo here to listen in, as you see, well, it's about her father and it might get a little awkward and you do know how I dislike awkwardness."

"I'm staying," Jo said, crossing her arms. If it was about her dad, she wanted to hear it.

"Oh my goodness, well, yes of course, if you must, dear." Mavis's brow was furrowed and she kept looking around furtively, as if she expected Nash to jump out at any second. "Well, Quin, dear, you know how I have owed our good friend Nash some money for a while?" She turned to John and whispered, "He loaned me money to fix my porch roof—there was nothing untoward about it—" and then turned back to Quin, "well, I paid him off with a family heirloom and I'm afraid I might, I may, I think I should not have done that? I was hoping you could help?"

"Was it Doors?" Quin asked bluntly.

"Oh my, yes," she said, trying to smile while glancing nervously at Jo. "I'm sure, well, you know—is there anything—?"

"We'll take her to a conference room," John interrupted, "and deal with this when we're done here. I'm sure we will have plenty of questions for you."

Terry stepped forward and took Ms. Oliphant's arm gently. "I'll take her to room DR-2B," she said. "Please come with me, ma'am."

John turned and pulled Quin and Jo the rest of the way through the crowd, to where a group of scientists huddled around a computer. One of them held a notebook and was scribbling rapidly, but the others were fixated on the screen in front of them.

"Sit here!" John ordered, dragging two chairs over.

The Door they had come out of—she assumed—stood nearby.

Then, without warning, one of the scientists shouted, "Now! Now!"

Everyone crowded around a computer screen and John wiggled his way to the front. Jo couldn't see what they were looking at, but John began narrating.

"The team has arrived in the neighborhood," he said. "They are taking position around the house."

A moment later he added, "They've taken out one guard—he's been captured."

Jo felt the muscles in her neck tighten as she clenched her jaw. This was her father they were talking about! That they were trying to catch! And it was partially her fault. Of course, they would have raided anyway, but she shouldn't have helped them. She was a terrible child. Though, to be fair, her father was a terrible father.

"They've caught a second guard," John said, interrupting her thoughts. "And a third. Now they're moving in to surround the house."

"The lead is taking down the front door, while her second is taking down the back."

"They've entered the house!"

Jo held her breath and squeezed her eyes shut. She found that she both wanted and didn't want to know what was going to happen. Quin touched her arm gently.

The scientists began murmuring and muttering to each other, so that Jo couldn't hear what they were saying.

"What's happening?" she heard Quin ask.

Jo opened her eyes to see John turn away from the computer. "There's no one there," he said. "The house is empty."

"Did you find the Doors?" Quin asked.

"Yes," John replied, "but Nash is gone."

CHAPTER 9

It was all ridiculous. He was here, with Jo Nash, because he had been abducted by a criminal and threatened with blackmail, and now he was stuck while a team that he should have been a part of was conducting a raid, and the criminal in question had somehow disappeared—and none of it made any sense whatsoever.

He stood up. He would go through and find Nash. What did it matter if he got in trouble? He was bored, miserable—all he wanted to do was take unnecessary risks. So why not take one now? It was just another gamble—this time, his career would be on the line.

"What are you doing?" John demanded, looking over his shoulder at Quin.

"Wait," one of the scientists said. "Something is happening!"

Quin paused.

"They're here!" the scientist exclaimed. "They stepped out of one of the Doors!"

"No!" John yelled at the screen. "Go, go, go!"

"Who are you talking to?" Quin leaned in. He saw the police officers running towards Nash and Mason, but then the two criminals turned and jumped through the Door that led to the swamp.

"Why aren't they following?" John moaned, grabbing his hair and pulling.

"They're not qualified," Quin said calmly. He felt a sudden rush of excitement. He was qualified. He could go. He could fix this.

John knew it too. "Then you go! Or else they'll escape!" he exclaimed. He turned to the side, grabbed a hover cam, and handed it to Quin "Go! Go!"

"You sure?" Quin asked, taking the cam from John.

"Just go!" one of the other scientists shouted. She pushed him in the direction of the Door. "They're getting away!"

Quin held out his hand to Jo. She took it without question, and he stepped forward, pulling both of them through the Door. He could hear John yelling as the noise and confusion melted away.

"You wait here," he whispered to her, and then turned to the officers that stood looking helplessly at the three Doors in Mason's living room. "I'm a qualified agent sent by John," he stated, and then jumped through the next Door into the swamp.

He landed knee-deep in swamp juice with bugs buzzing and swirling around his face. Nash and Mason were already a notable distance ahead of him, slogging through the weeds and mud. He activated the hover cam and stepped forward, his feet sinking deeper into the mud with every step.

"Hold up!" Quin shouted. "You're under arrest!"

"Where did you come from?" Nash demanded, looking over his shoulder at Quin with a startled expression.

"You're under arrest!" Quin shouted again.

"Dammit," Nash said, barely loud enough for Quin to hear. "We had better move faster."

"I said, stop!"

"They're going to find those photos!" Nash called over his shoulder. "You should probably go back and try to hide them before you get fired."

"I won't get fired if I bring you in," Quin stated, trying to pick up his pace. Moving through the swamp was difficult enough—roots and vines tripped him, mud threatened to suck him under, and water soaked into his clothes, weighing him down—but trying to move rapidly was even harder. He was impressed at Nash and Mason's speed, but he knew it was only a matter of time before he caught up.

Then he heard a splash a short distance behind him. He turned to see Jo almost up to her waist in the mud.

"What are you doing here?" he demanded.

"I'm not letting that tramp get away! She tried to kill my dad! And she did kill Stanky!"

"Well," Quin called, "I'm not waiting for you."

"No need," Jo replied, slogging towards her left. Quin frowned. She was taking a shortcut to the wooden path. On one hand, that was a great idea. On the other, what if they turned, went a different way? He shook his head and kept moving. He didn't want to lose them.

Sweat—or was it mud?—dripped from his forehead into his eyes. He pushed as hard as he could through the water, listening to the couple argue ahead of him.

"You're abysmal at planning!" Mason accused. "If you hadn't been so gung ho to visit that Oliphant lab, we would have known the cops were coming. We would have been able to get out! It wasn't even that great!"

"They took out our guards!" Nash argued. "We never would have seen them coming, and we would have gotten caught! Going to that weird lab place is the only reason we had a chance to get through to here."

"Yeah, like this place is so good," Mason said. "We're up to our ears in mud and *still* being chased by a cop! A cop that *you* invited into *my* house, I might add! If we ever get out of this, I'm ditching you. Going off on my own! You've never been good for me."

Quin shook his head. How Nash had managed to stay out of the grips of the law for so long was beyond him. Especially with someone like Mason as his second-in-command.

Nash swatted a bug that had landed on his neck, and Mason began to laugh, a deep hearty laugh that resonated in the swamp. It had begun—the plants had started to work their charms. Nash joined her in laughter, and Quin could even feel a chuckle begin bubbling up in his abdomen. But he focused on keeping his mind clear, on reaching his target—he had to catch them.

A few minutes later, their laughter dissipated.

"Ugh, this is awful," Mason complained. It was terrible, Quin noted, to be just far enough behind them to not catch them, but still have to listen to everything they said.

"It's a swamp," Nash said. "What did you expect?"

"Yeah, but really, what are we doing?" Mason asked. She pulled herself up an over a log, disturbing a frog that ribbited and dove into the mud. "We should go home. This isn't going to help us or save us. At most, it's only going to delay the inevitable. I want to go back."

"You can go back," Nash replied, "but I'm not." He gestured over his shoulder to Quin. "And I have a feeling he's not going anywhere either."

Quin wanted to go home too. The difference was, he knew it was an effect of the plants, and not a real feeling. "You should go back!" he called out, slapping at a bug that had settled in for dinner on his bald scalp. "It's fruitless to try to escape!"

"Hear that?" Nash said. "He's trying to discourage us. Pick up the pace!"

And they did. Quin sighed to himself. They were both smaller than him, and lighter, and somehow were able to go even faster than they had been. Quin was sick of swamps and he wasn't sure he had much left to give.

After a few minutes, he heard Mason ask, "What's that?" and realized they had reached the wooden path. Quin put in extra effort to move more quickly through the water and roots as they climbed up and began to jog down the trail. A moment later, they were out of sight. Quin didn't hesitate. As soon as he reached the wooden path, he heaved himself up onto it. He began to run, his feet pounding against the wooden slats and leaving a wet trail behind him. If the police followed them through, they would know where he had gone. Probably.

This was what he needed, he decided after a few minutes of running. A nice jog, and an easy manhunt. Something to make him feel like he had some kind of purpose, a little adrenaline, and a good cardio workout. The heat and humidity of the swamp made him sweat buckets, and he could feel a little of the tension and stress from earlier in the day dripping off, too. He had begun to feel good, in fact, and was almost having fun.

The swamp suddenly ended, and the great green hill with all the cabins on it opened up in front of him. Nash and Mason were halfway up the hill, heading for the farthest house.

"Not the orange one," Quin muttered to himself.

He began to run as fast as he could, and then saw Jo running from the opposite side of the hill. She had somehow managed to loop around this clearing. He was only halfway up the hill when Mason and Nash made it into the house and slammed the doors shut behind them. He knew they would immediately begin putting furniture in front of the door to try to keep it shut.

"What do we do?" Jo asked as she ran up to him. She stopped for a moment and gasped for air.

"Go through a window," Quin replied, striding around the cabin to one side. Sure enough, there was a window—already broken.

"Isn't this the rage house?" Jo asked, a worried expression on her face.

"Yes," Quin said. "I think you should stand back. I'll go in and bring them out, but at least one of us should try to stay unaffected by anger."

"Okay," Jo said. "I'll only come in if you need help."

Quin crawled through the broken window and saw that the inside of this house was in awful condition. The walls were littered with holes, and nearly every piece of furniture was broken. Shreds of eviscerated pillows covered the room, and so many feathers lay all over it looked like someone had murdered a flock of geese. There were scratches in the wooden paneling, and the curtains hung in tatters. He could hear Nash and Mason shouting at each other from another room.

"It's your fault!" Mason screamed. "If you hadn't been so stupid, so *greedy*, we never would have gotten into this mess! All we needed to do was wait to look through the Doors. If we had waited, we could have done it safely, smartly! Or better yet, if you had taken *actual money* from that batty old lady, then we could be rebuilding your empire now, not getting chased through a god-awful swamp by the police!"

"You're blaming me?" Nash bellowed. "You're the one who decided it was a good idea to blackmail *Quin Black* into paying us back for a game that the police interrupted! If he hadn't come around, they would probably never have found us. He works for the military, for Ivanna the Bard's sake!"

"You should have never let him play your games in the first place! What kind of idiotic moron lets a guy from the military into his illegal gambling night?"

"He's an easy mark!" Nash yelled back. "Rich! And always wasting his dad's money!"

"That's not true!" Quin yelled, stepping out into the room. He could feel all of his anger boiling over. His frustration at his career, which seemed to be going nowhere; his annoyance with John always nagging him about making better choices; his deep unfulfilled desire to do something meaningful with his life instead of doing busywork for the Globe—it all began to bubble up like a pot about to overflow in white foam and rage.

Without quite realizing what he was doing, he launched himself forward towards Nash—but miscalculated and barely grazed him, instead landing face-first on the floor. The pain felt good, like he had just woken up, and he grinned as he stood, staring Nash down. He swung his fist, which connected squarely with Nash's nose.

"STOP!" Mason yelled, leaping onto Quin's back.

Quin spun around, using Mason to knock Nash off his feet. Nash lay sprawled on the floor, a stunned look on his face. Then,

Quin pulled Mason up over his head and threw her onto the ground. She landed hard and groaned as the air rushed out of her lungs. Quin bent down angrily, resisting the urge to punch both of them in the face as hard as he could—repeatedly—and instead, grabbed them by their shirts and dragged them out the back door of the cabin.

Jo was waiting, her muscles tense and a frown on her face. Quin knew he must look a little intimidating—he was breathing like a bull and more furious than he had ever been in his life.

"Open the door!" he shouted.

Jo ran across the grass as quickly as she could as Quin pulled Nash and Mason behind him. They both squirmed, but now clear of the rage house, hopefully realized that picking a fight with an enraged Quin Black was a bad idea. Quin could feel his own anger beginning to recede, and he took deep breaths of the outside air to help calm himself and clear the skap out of his system.

He dragged the two into the contentment house and threw them both on a couch in the living room. He felt a calm start to come over himself, and welcomed it.

Jo sat down in a chair facing her father and Mason, and crossed her arms.

Quin stood to one side, noticing as the hover cam came to settle in beside him.

Jo cut right to the chase.

"You tried to kill my dad," she said, pointing to Mason.

Mason's jaw dropped. "That's ridiculous!" she exclaimed. "I did... no such... no such..." She was having trouble lying, Quin could see. The contentment house made it hard to tell anything but the truth—when you were truly content, there was no reason for lies, after all, right?

"You tried to kill my dad," Jo said again, this time more calmly and with even more confidence.

Nash looked at Mason quizzically. "Did you?"

"I... I..." Mason shut her mouth stubbornly. If she were unable to lie, then she would simply not talk.

"It makes sense," Nash said calmly, leaning back against the couch.

"It does?" Jo asked. "Why? Why does it make sense?"

"She tried to get me to take out an insurance policy on myself," he said, his eyes drooping ever so slightly. He must be tired, Quin thought. He had used up a lot of energy trudging through the swamp and fighting with Mason in the rage house. Then Quin's own exhaustion hit him like a weighted fist. He'd had quite the day, between slogging through swamps all morning, almost falling off a mountain, getting kidnapped and blackmailed, and then running through more swamps and participating in a police raid. He decided to sit down, too. He could always catch up to them if they tried to run away.

"How much?" Jo asked.

"One and a half million," Nash responded. "She wanted at least fifty percent to go to her." He gave a short laugh. "Joke's on her though—I set it up so it all went to you, Jo."

"Wow," Jo said, her eyebrows raising. "That might be the nicest thing you've ever done for me."

"I can't believe you would do that to me," Mason said in a flat tone of voice. She was frowning slightly, head leaning back against the couch. "I've been there for you from the moment I met you! I've helped you run dozens of scams, hundreds of gambling nights. I've collected from thousands of people, broken fingers and arms, even killed for you!"

"I did tell you not to do that last one," Nash said, holding up his finger. "Guy didn't actually need to die—just deserved it."

"Wait," Quin broke in. "You can't believe he wouldn't make his insurance payout to you? But you tried to kill him…"

"Yeah," Jo agreed. "Logic definitely seems off there."

"It doesn't matter," Nash said, shaking his head. "I never would have had the money go to Mason. I only keep her around to do my dirty work for me, and for some fun. You were always the most important person to me, Jo."

"Then why won't you let me go?" she asked. "Why won't you let me go to school and do what I want with my life? I want to be free!"

He shrugged. "You're all I have left of your mother, you know that? If you leave, I'm left with nothing. I want you to be happy, but I want you to be happy with me. You're my family."

Quin felt like he was sinking into his chair. This was the most comfortable house he had ever been in. He thought it might be worth it to stick around, to stay for a while. One part of his mind was arguing that no, this was bad, that he should get out as soon as possible, but the chair was so comfortable, and the house so peaceful and calm. Why go anywhere? Why do anything? All of his anger and frustration, rage and dissatisfaction with life drained out of him. He liked this feeling. He liked being content.

"That's sweet, Nash," Jo said. She too was leaning back in her chair, drowsily, enjoying the peace of the room.

"I feel like I should be more upset than I am," Mason said, looking at Nash. "You took me off the streets and then betrayed me—but I think I understand. I should not have tried to kill you."

"How'd you do it?" Nash asked.

She shrugged. "Your brother helped me. We figured if you both died, then he would get some of the insurance payout too."

"Also, they're cheating together," Jo added sleepily.

"Well," Nash said without even raising his voice. "That was very unkind of you. Both of you."

"I apologize," Mason said. "Can you ever forgive me?"

"I think so," Nash said, "but we're done after this. There is no more you and me—it will be me and Jo from now on. Father and daughter."

Mason took a deep breath, a tear forming in one eye. "I understand. But I think I need to be alone for a few minutes." She stood up. "I'll be right outside."

There was something wrong with this scenario, Quin knew, but he couldn't quite grasp what it was. She shouldn't be sad—he knew

84

that. Her own poor choices had caused the situation. In fact, she was almost entirely to blame for everything. She started this entire chain of events when she blew up Nash's house. But there was something else wrong too. What was it? Slowly, a thought wiggled its way into his mind—Mason was going outside, but it was so calm, so peaceful in here. Why would she do that? Why would she leave? But it didn't matter. She would come back in—he knew it. She would see that it was much nicer in here than out there, much calmer, a perfect place to be.

"You two look like you're about to fall asleep," Nash said.

"It's so nice here," Jo said, smiling lazily at her father. "When we were here last time, we almost decided to stay."

"You were here before?" Nash asked.

"Of course," Jo said. "We lied to you about it."

"Why?" Nash pressed, a barely perceptible frown on his forehead.

"This is Nalada," Quin said very slowly. "The plants here drug you with rage and laughter and sadness and longing. We didn't want you to introduce emotion drugs to Pomegranate City."

"Ah yes," Nash said, nodding slowly. "I see how that could be a good way of making money. But don't worry, Jo. I forgive you, now that I know." He sat forward in his chair. "I am worried about Mason—I think I will go check on her."

"We'll be right here," Quin said, leaning his head back against the chair. Everything else melted away, except the comfort of the chair and the peacefulness of the room around him. His annoyance of having to trudge through the swamps now seemed trivial, and his need for excitement and adrenaline faded away. His discontentment with life felt as though it had happened years ago, instead of hours. His urge to gamble faded too, and a quiet, wonderful emptiness swirled through his mind. All he wanted was to sit here, with Jo, and maybe sleep.

But then another memory swam into his consciousness—an image of John, red-faced, yelling at Quin. "I thought you were my best friend!" he had yelled. "But maybe you're too stupid to be my friend!" Quin knew that insulting someone's intelligence was the worst insult John could ever give to anyone. He felt a twinge of guilt for hurting John, for making him so angry, for betraying him. He should apologize, and then maybe bring him here to experience this wonderful place where all of his troubles melted away.

Quin sat up slowly.

"Jo," he said.

"Hmmm."

"I have to go find John and apologize to him."

She nodded. "He was really mad."

"Do you want to come?" he asked.

"I guess so." She shrugged. "Can we come back though?"

Quin nodded. "I'd like that."

They stood together, and Quin felt a little dizzy, like he was slightly drunk. They strolled casually outside and looked around. Mason and Nash weren't outside, where Quin had thought they'd be. He looked around, confused.

"Where did they go?" he asked Jo. He took a few deep breaths, trying to clear his head, and looked around. The dizziness faded slowly.

"There's Mason," she said casually, pointing towards the wooden trail that looped around the hill. She was running back towards the Door. "And there's Nash." He was running in the opposite direction, deeper into the planet.

"Oh no," Quin said. Comprehension rushed back into his head. They were getting away. He was supposed to be catching them, but they had a head start in opposite directions.

"I'll take Mason," Jo said, her eyes alert once more. Without hesitating another moment, she scurried down the hill towards the swamp.

"I guess I'll take Nash," Quin said, and once again, he began to run.

This run was different than the last. He took gasps of air as full as he could, hoping that the air here was clean enough to clear the remaining contentment out of his lungs. He couldn't believe how powerful the drug in that house had been—he had been ready to stay there forever and never leave. He was grateful that John's anger had provided the niggling sense of guilt that had dragged him up off his couch. Otherwise, he would still be there right now, dreaming of nothing, dying of contentment. And so would Jo.

The more he breathed the outside air, the better he felt. He knew there was still a risk of him inhaling the flowers' perfume as he ran, but at least out here the air was free to move, and he wasn't breathing distilled essence of emotion—only getting whiffs of it as he went. And running was good too. He would metabolize more oxygen and move past potential dangerous areas much more quickly.

The wooden trail curved through the trees. Nash had quite the head start, but Quin could hear his feet pounding against the boards in the distance. All Quin needed to do was slowly close the gap, one step at a time. He poured all of his energy, all of his willpower into his legs and feet, feeling his muscles flex and burn, feeling the sweat roll down his skin in rivers, feeling his breath rip through his mouth into his lungs. He felt exhilarated, fulfilled, alive—for the first time in a long while.

The swamp around him slowly became more and more deciduous, less muddy, with more ground shrubs and less groundwater. He seemed to be going up at a slight incline, and he saw fewer and fewer of the skap plants. That was a relief. Then more and more coniferous trees appeared, mixed in with the deciduous, and he was decidedly out of the swamp. The bugs began to leave him be, and the smells here were more familiar—similar to the forests on Sagitta, to the forests of Earth.

Then Quin burst out into an opening, and the world gave way around him as the wooden trail rose up, up away from everything, now a narrow bridge spanning a gorge that plunged down hundreds of feet to where a tiny river gurgled and rushed, slowly carving the rock deeper and deeper. Nash was almost across to the other side, but Quin had to pause for a minute as a wave of dizziness rushed over him, no doubt an aftereffect of contentment.

He took a few deep breaths and then began to slowly jog, in awe of the beauty around him, but also careful to focus on the bridge so as not to lose his sense of balance. He was almost on Nash—he wouldn't get away now, unless Quin was stupid and fell off the bridge.

When he reached the other side, the wooden path continued, leading him through a narrow pass in the small mountain range. The temperature cooled slightly as he moved into the mountains, and he found it refreshing. The air smelled wonderful and clean on this side of the gorge. He estimated that he had run nearly three miles.

Then the mountain pass ended and Quin skidded to a halt as he rounded a corner. In front of him spread a small city, with a spire rising high into the air in the center and houses upon houses stretching out from it in a neat wheel. The flag that hung on the spire was tattered navy and gold, and from here on the wooden path turned to asphalt—first a parking lot filled with old, rusted vehicles, and then a road. Quin was surprised to see so many vehicles when he didn't see any people on the trail. Perhaps they had simply gone a different way than he had come from.

Nash was already partway down the road, but Quin could tell that he was tiring. Four miles was a long way to go, and Nash wasn't young anymore; plus, Quin doubted he ran as a regular form of exercise. Nash would have to stop or walk soon to rest. That was when Quin would catch him—unless Nash found a good place to hide. If he made it into the city far enough ahead of Quin, then he could turn down any number of streets, blend in with the people, or hide in a house or behind a building. Quin might never find him.

Again he picked up his pace. He narrowed his eyes and focused on the moving figure of Nash, and Quin ran as though his life depended on it.

But Nash reached the city before Quin and disappeared into the buildings.

Quin pushed all of his remaining energy, all of his willpower into his muscles and ran as fast as he could, his feet pounding against the pavement, straight into the city, the direction Nash had taken. He ran by more rusted vehicles and house after house until he arrived at the spire in the center. If he had to search the entire city, he would start here and work his way out.

To his surprise, he found Nash standing silently, staring at the spire. It rose up over the city on four legs, a patterned staircase curving up the middle. At the bottom was a pile of bones.

Quin spun to look around him and realized what his brain had not connected before—the city was dead. The vehicles hadn't been used in decades; the houses were empty. He saw no people, felt no movement, heard no sounds. They stood in an empty city, and in the center rose a pile of bones. From it, a plant grew, its leaves and tendrils poking through the eye sockets of the skulls, wrapped around arm and leg bones, making a ladder of the rib cages. The plant had probably had ample fertilizer as the bodies decayed.

"What... what happened?" Nash asked, his eyes wide, mouth agape.

"They're dead," Quin replied, not even thinking about the inanity of his comment.

"Yes," Nash said. "What happened?"

Quin walked to the nearest house and opened the door, peering in. Inside were four more skeletons, sitting on their couches. At the next house, one of the bodies lay on the floor, and two others sat in chairs. In the back yard, three more bodies sat comfortably, as if they had simply died as the sun set and not moved since.

He stepped back out into the park in the middle of the city and stared up at the metal spire.

"They're dead," he said again.

Then he stepped forward and looked more closely at the plant. He saw that it had green speckles on its leaves and green buds opening slowly, about to bloom.

"Of contentment," he finished.

"A whole city?" Nash said.

"A whole city," Quin replied.

Nash looked around him and then turned to Quin. "I think you had better get me out of here," he said. "I don't want to die here, too." He looked exhausted. "But it's miles back to the Door."

"No," Quin said, "actually I don't think so." He pointed past the spire, at a tall building on the other side of the city. The sign, barely visible from where they stood, read "Hemen Temple of Feeling."

"What's that?" Nash asked.

"That's our exit," Quin replied. He gripped Nash's arm tightly enough to leave bruises, and began to stroll down the road that led towards the temple. The wind howled, and the trees creaked as they swayed. He listened for any sign of life at all, but it was still as empty as it had been this morning—no sounds of laughter or conversation, of construction or moving vehicles—nothing.

When they finally reached the temple, he led Nash up the steps slowly, and turned to look out over the city one last time. It was eerie knowing the reason the city had died. It was strange, knowing that he could have been one of them.

"Let's go," he said, guiding Nash through the temple. His feet still echoed eerily in the silence. Skeletons still sat contentedly in the chairs, staring ahead. The Door still glittered on the dais. He led Nash up to it, and they stepped through, the dead city drifting into darkness behind them.

CHAPTER 10

Jo shook off the effects of the drug as quickly as she could as she followed Mason through the swamp. She had no idea how she was going to get Mason through the Door—it wasn't as if Jo was stronger than her father's ex-girlfriend. But she was going to do everything she could to catch the woman who attempted to murder her father to prison, once and for all.

The bugs buzzed around her head and the swamp gases smelled awful, and Jo decided that once the day was over and she had made it home, she was never going to a swamp again. They were too wet, too humid, too buggy, too smelly. She felt a little bit of laughter bubble up inside her, and she pushed it back. There was no way she was going to let the skap take over her mind again.

Mason hadn't left the trail yet, so Jo followed her at a distance, wondering if she even knew how to get back to the Door at all, or if she was just running aimlessly, hoping that she would eventually arrive. Finally, when Mason had run by both of the spots where Jo would have climbed off the trail to get to the Door, she called out, "Hey! Do you know where you're going?"

"Shut up!" Mason yelled back.

"I'm just saying, if you're trying to go back to Pomegranate City, you missed the route."

"How would you know?" Mason spit back.

"I've been here before? That's how?" Jo rolled her eyes. Mason was kind of thick.

Mason slowed a little and a moment later Jo caught up to her.

"I want to go home," Mason said, looking stressed. "I don't like it here. I don't want to be here. I miss not being in a swamp, I miss my friends, I miss my house, and I want to start over without you or your dad, on my own—*and not here!*"

"I can help with that," Jo said, shrugging.

"How do I know you're not going to lure me out into the wilderness and dump me?" Mason asked, frowning.

Jo shrugged. "Because I want to go home too." She found, to her surprise, that it was true. It wasn't just that she wanted to be out of this swamp, it was that she wanted to be home. She missed her favorite coffee shops and her friends from school, she missed her dad's house (that was now blown up) and she missed the way Pomegranate City smelled, the hustle and bustle, the lights and the busyness. "I want to go home too," she repeated.

"Alright," Mason said. "Let's go."

Jo led her back to the spot on the trail that ended closest to the Door, and jumped into the water. Mason followed her, and they spent the next ten minutes slogging through the mud. Jo was tired of being wet, tired of being muddy, tired of being eaten by bugs, and just tired in general. She would be happy to get home.

The Door appeared in the swamp before them, and Jo sighed gratefully. She would be glad to be back on solid ground. She stepped through with Mason on her heels.

"Aw fudge lizards," Mason muttered. "I forgot about the cops."

A round of cheers went up as the officers from the raid ran forward to slap cuffs on Mason. Jo quickly found herself besieged by scientists, all asking her a thousand questions. Only one question stood out to her from the bunch. It was John, his eyes wide and worried.

"Where's Quin?" he asked. "Please tell me—where's Quin?"

She grinned tiredly at him. "He's chasing down my dad," she replied, and then gestured towards the couch. "Do you all mind if I sit down?"

"Please!" John exclaimed. "Out of the way, out of the way!" He guided her to the couch, waving the police officers that surrounded the Doors back. Officer Reynolds came to sit down on the coffee table facing her.

"Quin got the whole thing on the hover cam," Jo told her. "Mason confessed to everything." She was so exhausted she could barely muster up the energy to put on her confident face, but she tried, and gave Officer Reynolds a little smile.

"What about Quin?" John asked again fiddling with his tie. It looked like it had orange spiders all over it. "The last thing I told him was that he was too stupid to be my friend." He put his face dramatically into his hands and moaned, "I'm a horrible person!"

"He chased after Nash," Jo said, "but they ran in the opposite direction of the Door, so I don't know how long it will take. And don't worry, Quin didn't take it to heart. He was actually talking about coming back to apologize to you when he ran off after Nash."

"Apologize?" John looked up from his hands. "That doesn't sound like him."

Jo gave a small tired smile. "It's a long story," she said.

"If you don't mind," Officer Reynolds said, "what exactly did Mason confess to?"

"She tried to kill my dad," Jo replied simply.

"And she just… admitted it? Why?"

"We were kind of, well, drugged," Jo said, "I think? But it was by accident. Nobody did it to us on purpose."

At that moment, a noisy group of scientists burst into the room carrying computer equipment, boxes of tools, and a variety of other things that Jo didn't recognize. They chattered excitedly, and the noise in the room went from a quiet murmur to a loud babble.

"Jo, Officer Reynolds," John said, "why don't you come back to the Globe with me? I have Mavis Oliphant in a conference room there, and she claims to know something about the Doors. We can talk with her while we wait for Quin to get back."

"That would be wonderful," Officer Reynolds said. "Is that okay with you, Jo?"

Jo looked at Mason who was being spoken to by another police officer. "She's not going to get away again, right?" Jo asked. "Because I'll chase her down again if I have to. I'll shoot her in the knees."

"I think we've got it handled," Officer Reynolds said kindly.

"Okay then," Jo stood up slowly from the couch, still dripping, and followed John through the third Door.

The Door Room was much quieter this time. A few scientists still buzzed about, but the general commotion had significantly decreased. It was after hours, and the room felt much larger and more echoey than before.

Jo followed John across the floor, looking about curiously. Every single one of these Doors led to another place, another world, with different people and different plants, different animals and a different sky. It was really incredible to think about. She could go anywhere, just by popping through, and come back one, two, three minutes later. To see worlds in a blink of an eye, to explore the universe in a heartbeat—it was amazing.

John pushed open the door to conference room DR-2B, and Mavis sat there drinking a cup of tea, a tiny, old, wrinkly lady in a big chair.

"There you are," Mavis said, smiling a timid smile. "I thought you had gone and forgotten me."

"Of course not, Ms. Oliphant," John said kindly, sitting next to her. "This is Officer Reynolds. She is investigating Andrew Nash's operation."

"Hello there," Mavis said, giving a little wave. "Nice to meet you."

"John tells me you have some information for us," Officer Reynolds asked. "Mind if I record the conversation?"

"Oh well, I suppose not," Mavis replied, sighing. "I'm a bit old to get in too much trouble, I suppose."

"Go ahead," Officer Reynolds said.

"Well, there's not that much to tell," Mavis said. "But I guess you could say that I owed Nasty Nash some money—he loaned me for fixing my porch, you understand—and I paid it back with family heirlooms. But I didn't really think about it, you know? And then I started to remember, remember that maybe I shouldn't have done that. Maybe those heirlooms would be best forgotten. So I came to my dear friend, Quin—where is he?—to ask for help, but it seems like it might be a rather busy day for him."

"What were these family heirlooms?" Officer Reynolds asked.

"Why, Doors, of course," Mavis said. "I know they were illegal to have, so I thought maybe I should give them up, give them away, but I had forgotten, forgotten the rules, you see. And I had found them in an old trunk where I also found my old, old diary, from the year my father died, you understand, and I remember he said to me, 'Mavis, keep these Doors safe,' and I wrote it in my journal too, I wrote, 'Mavis, keep these Doors safe.'"

"Did you write anything else in your journal?" John asked. "About where the Doors came from? Or why your father wanted you to keep them safe?"

"Well, yes," Mavis said, "I have the journal right here, if you'd like to see it. Please don't read the whole thing, but if you look on the 5th of February, it will tell you."

John opened the book to the bookmarked page and read aloud:

"I think Father is going to die soon. Today he gave me three Door cylinders and told me that under no circumstances should I part with these Doors. He told me to protect them, for they could be the undoing of everyone, including me. He said, 'Mavis, keep these Doors safe.' He told me that two of the Doors had been given to him as an inheritance when his uncle, Lake Oliphant, disappeared, presumed dead, and that the other I shouldn't like to know the reasons why. But I don't much care. What is a Door to me? I can't use them and I can't sell them and I can't give them away—so I suppose I shall stash them in a trunk until my dying day. But dear future Mavis, if you're reading this, just remember, keep them safe."

"Please, stop reading there," Mavis said. "The next account gets a little…" she grinned, "…personal."

John closed the book. "Lake Oliphant? Which two Doors are his?"

"If I had to guess," Jo said, "the swamp and the lab."

"The lab?" John's face perked up.

She nodded. "You'll have to have Quin take you there."

"If you don't mind," John asked, "who exactly was your father?"

"Oh, you might remember him," Mavis said, waving a hand in the air. "Cares Oliphant. He had a motto—*Cares Cares!*"

"I remember him!" John said. "He was running for the office of Administrative Chair but had to drop out because he grew ill. That was shortly before he passed, right?"

"Yes, yes," Mavis said.

"Mavis," Officer Reynolds asked. "May I ask you a personal question?"

"Please, dear," Mavis replied, turning to face the police officer.

"Is it possible that you personally were involved in gambling at Nash's establishment?"

Mavis shook her head and tsked. "Now honey, someone as old as me would be mighty foolish to be getting involved in that."

Jo kept her mouth shut. She didn't want to get Mavis in trouble, though she knew that Mavis' inclination for gambling was pretty severe. She had lost a lot of money when she frequented Nash's secret events.

"We know you have," John cut in. "Quin meets up with you to get locations for illegal—" John slapped a hand over his mouth. He had inadvertently outed Quin.

"What did you say?" Officer Reynolds asked. She stared John down. "Did you imply that Quin Black has something to do with Nash's illegal gambling and hasn't brought the information to the police?"

Jo gulped. She didn't want Quin to get in trouble—not since he had saved her and offered to help rat out Mason then spilled his soul

96

to her at the contentment house—and since she had told him everything, too! She swallowed and put on her confident face, the best version that she could muster, and added a soothing tone to her voice.

"No, no," Jo cut in. "What John was saying is that Quin has tried to get Mavis to leak Nasty Nash's locations, but Mavis is a closed book. Which my dad always appreciated, you understand. But Mavis has—occasionally—showed up to some of our events. For a drink and to mingle, you understand. Not to play."

"And you would know this how?" Officer Reynolds asked. "Are you now confessing?"

"All I will admit to," Jo said cautiously—she didn't want to get herself in trouble either, "was that until I became of age, my father occasionally asked me to sit in and watch his guests. Keep an eye out for, well, any illegal activity. To keep things aboveboard."

She could tell Officer Reynolds didn't believe a word of it. "I see. So Mavis, you have occasionally visited Nasty Nash's establishment—but done nothing illegal—and Quin has tried to get the times and locations from you, but you refused."

"Oh yes, yes," Mavis agreed hastily, "that seems like it could all make sense."

Jo shook her head. Mavis was not good at this.

"Okay," Officer Reynolds said, shaking her head and sighing. "Here's the thing. I'm not trying to catch you, Mavis, or even you, Jo. I only need evidence to put Nasty Nash away. I know you both have some, and I am especially interested to hear what you know, Jo."

"That's a tall order," Jo said, crossing her arms, "asking me to betray my own dad like that. Assuming I know anything at all. Why would I do that?" She sniffed in pretend derision. The truth was, two hours ago, she would have gladly ratted out her father. But since his confessions in the house of contentment—he really did love and care about her—she wasn't sure she wanted to.

Officer Reynolds stood up and leaned forward, almost nose to nose with Jo. It was an intimidation tactic, one that Jo recognized, and she wouldn't let it work on her. She straightened her back and strengthened her resolve. After all the lizard's innards she had been through today, she wasn't about to let one police officer intimidate her into confessing the illegal things she had done, which by the way, had nothing to do with the situation at hand!

"Now see here," Officer Reynolds said. "If you are in any way impeding an investigation—"

She was interrupted as the door to the conference room burst open. In the doorway, Quin stood with the hover cam by his shoulder, dripping with sweat and tightly gripping Nash's arm. Nash looked around the room and saw Officer Reynolds staring down Jo. His eyes opened in mild panic. Jo hardly had time to process his facial expression when he blurted out, "It was me! Whatever Jo was confessing to, it was me!"

Jo raised her eyebrows and her jaw dropped. She blinked in shock, unable to maintain the confident demeanor she had been working so hard on. It was true. Her dad did love her after all, like he had said in the contentment house. Or maybe his visit to Nalada had really changed him. Either way, it made her love her dad a little bit more.

CHAPTER 11

Quin was tired. He had been questioned by multiple detectives and police officers, gone through a decontamination process, and nearly nodded off more than once. It was past midnight, and John was supposed to come walk home with him—which was good as he wasn't sure he could manage much more tonight.

"Hey." John poked his head into the room where Quin waited. "You ready?"

"Yeah," Quin said, dragging himself out of the chair.

They walked downstairs and out into the warm evening air. It was peaceful in the city this late, although towards downtown he could hear a noisy group making their way home from the bars. A light breeze drifted through the air. Quin felt calm, and the annoyed impatience with everything that had been plaguing him had quieted.

"So why was the last Door so important? The one that you had in the Door Room?" Quin asked after they had walked for a few minutes in silence. "Why did Mavis's father ask her to keep it safe?"

"Ah yes," John said, "an excellent question. Back when her father was in office, there was a huge scandal. The police raided a home on the word of a confidential informant and found not only drugs, but gambling, stolen valuables, and all kinds of other unsavory things. In the process of cleaning up, they confiscated a rather large number of Doors. Several of them led to the homes of prominent politicians or people in the city."

"Where did our Door lead?" Quin asked.

"No one knows," John replied, shrugging. "It was closed by the time the Globe tried to infiltrate it. It was suspected to be another high-ranking government official, presumably one who knew about the raid in question. But there were quite a few of those, and there was no other evidence."

"Why were you working on it now?" Quin asked.

"My assignment was to try to see if there was a way to track the location of closed Doors," John replied. "We were working with that one because it had an open case file on it. No other reason. But we know now—it led to a politician who was running for the office of Administrative Chair. That would have been a big scandal, back when he was alive."

They walked in silence as Quin contemplated the day. It had been long, there was no doubt about that. And he had been stupid, there was no doubt about that either. He would have to get his act together if he ever wanted to be done with sifting through uncategorized Doors and move on with his career. He felt extremely fortunate that nothing untoward had come out about his evening activities. It was miraculous, really.

"Hey John," Quin said, hesitantly.

"Yeah?"

"I wanted to say that you were right."

"About what?" John asked.

"I'm stupid," Quin replied. "Really stupid."

John punched him in the shoulder. "No you're not. You do dumb things sometimes, but I never should have said that. I was mad. I'm sorry."

"No, I deserved it," Quin said.

"I'm really glad you made it back okay."

John turned down a darkened street. The trees rustled in the night, and the shadows deepened around them. Quin frowned.

"Where are we going?" he asked.

John gestured to the end of the street. "Making a quick stop."

A moment later they stood in front of Mason's house. John flashed his Globe ID at the police officer on guard duty, and led Quin up the stairs. He flicked on the living room light and walked straight up to the middle Door. A moment later, he had vanished.

"I guess we're going through, then," Quin muttered, and followed John.

He nearly bumped into the scientist who stood agape as the robots greeted them. Quin blinked, trying to allow his eyes time to adjust from the darkness outside to the stark and blinding white light inside.

"It's amazing," John said, finally stepping forward as the robots guided them through the decontamination process.

Quin stayed quiet as they stepped out of the chambers and walked down the hallway. The door slid up and they stepped onto the hover platform.

John's jaw dropped as he gazed at the thousands of windows. "I... I..." he stuttered. "I didn't think this was possible!"

"What?" Quin asked.

"They're... they're... windows!"

"Yes, I can see that," Quin said.

John began to talk so fast Quin could hardly understand him. "It has been theorized by many different scientists that it would be possible to create a Door, and then somehow pin back the center, the curtain if you will, so that you could see through to the other side before you tried to step through it. The math was always somewhat out of reach, and no scientist I have ever known of has accomplished the task. These windows, while magnificent, are slightly different, in that you can't walk through them. If only we could study these, we could make more like them, we could probably..." He fell silent as the platform drifted past the window showing the Door Room.

"That's... the Globe," he whispered, pointing at one window, then the next, and the next. "And the Director's Office. That's the Oliphant museum—which used to be the Oliphant manor."

"Yes," Quin said. "It's how we knew Mason had tried to blow up Jo's dad. We saw Mason arguing with Jo's uncle through that window over—"

"Yes, yes," John interrupted, "but don't you see how dangerous this is? What if someone in the government got their hands on it?

Or a spy from another government or another planet? What if the higher ups in the Globe decided to use it to spy on their competitors, or to spy, well, on everyone? It'd be a disaster! There would be no privacy for anyone, ever!"

"I suppose you're right," Quin said, shrugging. That was essentially what Jo had been trying to tell him earlier in the day. Privacy, spying, conspiracy—it wasn't really what he felt like thinking about right now.

"That window into the Globe," John continued, "you can't see it from the other side. It's not there. I'll double check tomorrow, but I'm ninety-nine percent positive it's not there. And if it is there, it's been there for centuries and no one has noticed it. This is probably the most dangerous place I've ever been in." He shook his head back and forth, trying to comprehend the magnitude of the discovery.

"Lake Oliphant must have been a creeper," Quin muttered as the platform took them down, past thousands of windows, and into Oliphant's lair. John surprised Quin by bursting out laughing, but was quickly silenced by the beauty of the room they moved into.

"It's really wonderful," John breathed.

They strolled around the room, examining each of the windows that looked out onto beautiful scenery.

"That's where we were," Quin said, pointing to a window gazing down onto Nalada, high over the Hemen Temple of Feeling.

"This is really wonderful," John said again.

Quin led him over to Lake Oliphant's bones. John stared down at them solemnly. "He died in his castle, I guess."

"That he did," Quin replied.

They stayed for a few more minutes, looking through his bookshelves and some of the papers on his desk, and then headed back up towards the entrance.

"I think we should make this Door disappear all over again," John said quietly.

"Okay." Quin nodded.

"I brought an extra closed Door with me. It's in my bag, in Mason's living room."

"You planned this?" Quin asked, raising his eyebrows.

John shrugged. "I didn't know, but I had a feeling this might be something we might want to make disappear."

"You know that's illegal, right?" Quin asked.

"No," John said. "We won't keep it. We'll put it in the Globe, back in the massive piles of uncategorized Doors. You can categorize it wrong if you want—put 'DEAD PLANET' on it, or something. Then only you and I will know that it's there, hiding."

"I can do that," Quin replied.

They waved to the friendly robots, and stepped back through the Door into Mason's living room. To their surprise, Jo sat on the couch across from them, staring pensively at the Doors.

"What are you doing here?" John asked. "How did you get in?"

"Snuck in," she said. "I'm not a con man's daughter for nothing. What are you doing here?"

"I wanted to see the lab," John said. "It's beautiful. Absolutely beautiful."

"Yeah," Jo said, sighing softly.

"Don't tell anyone about it, okay?" John asked.

"Sure." She shrugged. "I was remembering the way it felt to be so calm, so at peace. The way I felt in the house of contentment." She looked up at Quin. "Do you think I'll ever feel that again?"

"Not the way it felt there," he replied. "But that wasn't real. That was a chemical affecting the way your brain processes the information around you. In real life, you'll find contentment eventually—you'll just have to work for it. Honestly, I think a lack of contentment is what drives us to keep going. It's what motivates us to work harder."

"Have you found it?" she asked.

Quin laughed. "Nope. But I'm less annoyed about everything than I was a day ago."

Jo nodded.

"You want us to walk you home?" John asked, gesturing towards the door.

Jo shook her head. "I think I'm going to find a floor to sleep on somewhere. Try to get to class on time tomorrow—hope I don't get arrested for anything."

"When you graduate from horticulture school," John said, "come find me. If you want to. We'll see if we can get you a job doing something interesting."

"Thanks," Jo said, grinning. She stood up from the couch, stepped forward, and gave Quin a hug. He held his arms out awkwardly, unused to shows of affection. She stepped back and grinned at him.

"You'll have to practice that," she said.

"I guess so," Quin replied.

"See you around." She waved and disappeared into the night.

"You got a hug!" John exclaimed delightedly, elbowing Quin in the ribs. "Well now, finally a girl who isn't afraid of you!" He bent down and began to wind the Door to Dr. Oliphant's lab into its cylinder.

"My commanding officer isn't afraid of me," Quin said grouchily. He carefully replaced the cylinder with the one John had grabbed from the Globe. It didn't look quite the same, but it was unlikely that anyone would notice.

"Yeah, but she doesn't count because she's your boss." John gave a little cheerful dance. "I can't wait to harass you about this for the rest of your life."

"Let's go," Quin said, holding open the door for his friend, "or I'm going to pass out and you'll have to drag me home."

"I'd leave you here," John retorted, grinning as he headed out into the street. "Goodnight, officer!" he called, waving as he adjusted the backpack that now held Lake Oliphant's secret lab.

"Night!" Quin also gave a quick wave and then smiled, to himself, in the dark. Finally, he was headed home, to sleep.

ACKNOWLEDGEMENTS

All In was the fastest book I've ever written and produced. I came up with the idea in June, wrote it in 2 weeks in July, and pushed through edits and publication in another month. This was partially because it's a novella length and was easier to write, and partly because of the crack team that helped me push through to the end.

First, I'd like to thank my mom, who, though she helps with every book, went above and beyond this time. She read four different versions of the book, all within a month. I can't imagine how boring it must have been, reading the same book over and over, with only slight alterations. Yet her feedback was absolutely invaluable, and I couldn't have done it without her.

Next, Mountains Wanted Publishing was able to do a copyedit in less than a week (despite that fact that I got my manuscript to her three days later than planned)! In addition, Zoe (as ever) jumped in and did a final white glove edit for me, helping me take the manuscript to the next level.

In addition, I'd like to thank Magpie Designs, LLC for creating yet another awesome-looking cover from my vague ideas, and without having read it.

Finally, Josh suffered through days of incessant talking about this book during the ideation, writing, and editing phases of the project. He provided his own ideas and take on the concept that helped me solidify what I wanted this book to be in such a short timeframe. He also came up with the title—or else the book would have no doubt been called something awful, like *The Moody Swamp*.

In short, I couldn't have done it alone.

Made in the USA
Middletown, DE
04 September 2017